A Nice Place to Live

A NOVEL

A Nice Place to Live

BY
ROBERT C. SLOANE

Crown Publishers, Inc.
New York

Printed in the United States of America

Published simultaneously in Canada by General Publishing Company Limited

Library of Congress Cataloging in Publication Data

Sloane, Robert C
A nice place to live.

I. Title.
PS3569.L594N5   813'.54   80-24740
ISBN: 0-517-542838 (cloth)
0-517-545152 (paper)

10 9 8 7 6 5 4 3 2 1

First Edition

To Fern
To Steve, Lori, Scott, and Sharon
To Betty and Sam who knew
To Señor Raymondo for his help

Let us ride the back of the Dragon,
Pull down the moon and the stars;
Let us enter the infinite darkness,
And partake of violence divine.

Nordic love poem

A Nice Place to Live

Prologue

The girl opened the corral gate and waited for the horse to saunter through it. She watched him quietly for a moment, then swung the gate closed and returned to the house.

The horse fed without enthusiasm, stamping his feet and breathing clouds of vapor into the damp March air. He suddenly lifted his head, shook it twice, and broke into a playful gallop around the edge of the corral, kicking his feet in high spirits. When he stopped, he lay down and began to dust his back and sides, trying to turn himself from one side to the other.

A flock of crows flew across his vision, forming a

noisy silhouette against the darkening evening sky. As the last echoes of their frightened departure died away, another sound came. It began as a deep, irregular panting and grew quickly to a roaring bellow that raged out of the brute maw of Chaos itself. As the volume increased, it became a thunder on the earth, that fractured the air, that caused the tall reeds standing by the shore to tremble. It persisted for several moments and then died away abruptly. And when it ended, a stillness settled on the scene, a stillness in which no birds flew, squirrels clung to branches, the wings of insects closed softly, immobile. Only a fox, its newly caught prey still struggling in its jaws, continued on its way through the salt-marsh grass.

The horse scrambled to his feet. His ears pressed forward. As he looked into the group of dark pine trees in front of him, the whites of his eyes began to show.

The horse lowered his head and whinnied. And then he wheeled on his hind legs, his hoofs churning the loose earth, and bolted. He ran, kicking viciously at something suddenly behind him. He was caught before he had crossed half the corral. He was dead a moment later. The manner of his death was, even under the harsh and savage laws of nature, an obscenity.

1

I t's perfect," Christine said, opening the station wagon door. "It's a perfect house, these are perfect grounds, that's a perfect tree."

"It's expensive," Nick growled from underneath his baseball cap.

Christine looked at him and shook her head. "Not only are Italians lousy lovers, but you know nothing about real estate values. This is a waterfront home on the North Shore of Long Island. Value. It's located in the Village of Mill Harbor. Swanky value. With a few subtle but distinctive touches, the house will double in value, probably by next week. What do you think, Joey?"

Joey Marino rested his eight-year-old chin on the car window ledge and surveyed the large old house and the ample grounds. Possibilities flooded his young mind: ball playing on the lawns surrounding the house, exploring in the nearby woods, fishing in the waters of Mill Harbor he saw shimmering in the distance. "This is better than Central Park," he said. "I think Mom is right. Can I look around?"

"Sure," Nick said. His eyes followed his son for a moment and then he turned to watch the tall figure of his wife walk toward the house. After ten years of marriage, Nick was still awed by her grace, her physical beauty. He watched the perfect thighs that swelled out from the jean shorts, the long, precisely cut blond hair that hung down to her shoulders, the fluid, proud way she moved her body. "Chris," he called. When she turned to him, he smiled in musing admiration. Christine Marino had a rare, indefinable beauty. The green eyes, the high cheekbones, the full mouth added up to more than their own perfection. Her features achieved a matchless amalgam of frailty and sensuality that still shook the heart of her husband.

Nick blinked once. "Kiddo," he said casually, "I think I'm really beginning to like you."

Christine smiled back at him and shook her head in mock sadness. It didn't work. Their eyes locked in love, the smiles disappeared from their faces.

It was Nick who broke the short silence. "You know, baby, I think I'll set up the bed first thing this afternoon."

"Yes," Christine said, her eyes still on his, "why

don't you do that." She turned once again toward the house. "And don't call me 'baby,'" she said, without turning around.

Nick tapped his forehead, looked up at the sky and walked to the loaded station wagon.

The furniture that had filled their Manhattan apartment was lost in the large rooms of the new house. Christine and Nick smiled as the moving men set their small table down in the large dining room. They winced at the one couch and two chairs that sat forlornly in the twenty-five-foot living room. "The moving men are *embarrassed*," Christine whispered.

But as they stood in the driveway and watched the van disappear, she turned to her husband. "Oh, Nick, it's heaven. I'm so happy I'm going to cry." She was jumping up and down trying to reach his lips when the clatter of horse's hoofs on the blacktop drew their attention. They looked at each other incredulously as a mounted figure, dressed totally in black from boots to flowing shirt, appeared around a bend in the driveway.

The tall, gaunt rider approached them, his piercing eyes staring out at them from his pale face.

"My God," Christine murmured, her hand seeking her husband's. "It's Dracula."

When the mounted figure was directly in front of them, he tried to dismount with his eyes locked into Christine's. His foot caught in the stirrup. As he struggled with it patiently, Nick squeezed Christine's hand to stop her from laughing.

"I don't believe this," he said softly. Christine started to laugh and put a hand to her mouth.

The rider gave up in defeat and sat straight in the saddle. "It seems," he said wearily, "that I am not coming down. My name is Maynard Drogin. Welcome to Mill Harbor."

"Well, thank you," Nick said. "Do you . . . live nearby?"

Drogin raised a thin arm. "I live in the old mill at the end of this cove. You can see it from here. That's how this town got its name. My family has owned most of the property on this side of the cove for generations. I'm in real estate myself."

Christine looked toward the square, dark structure a quarter of a mile away. "Was it really a mill?" she inquired.

"Yes, I fixed it up years ago. You'll have to come over sometime. Both of you. I've come with an invitation. Your neighbor, Karl Anderson, is having a cocktail party tomorrow evening. Sevenish. We all thought it would be nice for you to come and get to know your neighbors. Just follow the path along the shore. His is the first house you'll come to. Bring your son."

Nick and Christine looked at each other. Nick's eyes said, "I guess we'll have to sooner or later" and Christine's agreed.

"We'd love to," Nick said. "And thank you for welcoming us. It was thoughtful of you."

Drogin shrugged his shoulders. "That's what neighbors are for, are they not?" After an unsuccessful attempt to rear his horse, he wheeled around and rode away, shaking his entangled foot.

Nick looked at Christine. "Call the moving men," he

said. "We're going back to the city." Christine collapsed over the hood of the station wagon, her whole body convulsing with laughter. "My God," Nick shook his head, "he's right out of a bad vampire movie. He even *sounded* like Bela Lugosi. 'I'm in real estate myself.'"

Christine wiped the tears from her eyes. "Oh, Nick, he's so bad, he's wonderful."

"Yeah, but did you see the way he looked at you?" Nick put his arm around his wife's waist. "Well, the house has screens, anyway. If that doesn't keep him out, Sleazy will tear him to pieces." Together, they turned to look at their son's mongrel dog which was cowering inside the wagon, refusing to come out.

"Some watchdog *he* is," Christine laughed. "I could be attacked by a butterfly and he'd pretend to be asleep."

"You could also be attacked by something larger and prettier," Nick said, sliding his hand down to her buttock.

Christine looked up at the hard, handsome face of her husband. The black hair that fell down his forehead toward the bright blue eyes, the carved lips almost cruel in their arrogance.

"Nicholas, this is ridiculous," she said. "It's two o'clock in the afternoon, the house is an absolute mess. I don't even like you. I simply cannot stand insatiable Mediterranean types. I mean, really, forget it."

Nick drew her to him and kissed her.

"Nick, you are impossible. I want you to remove your hand from where it is, and . . ."

Nick kissed her again. Christine's arms went slowly around his neck. "Where's Joey?" she murmured.

"He's right there on the lawn. He's okay. Sleazy is watching him. From the car."

"Oh, great," Christine said.

"My antipasto," Nick said.

"My cannoli," she said.

"My chicken with lemon and garlic. My baklavás."

"Baklavás isn't Italian. It's Greek."

"I don't care," Nick crooned. "It's delicious. My manicotti."

Nick picked her up and carried her through the doorway. As always, when she felt the strength of him, she had difficulty breathing.

"I love you," she said quietly.

"Of course you do," was his answer.

At the end of the lawn that sloped away from the house toward the patch of dark trees, Joey Marino stood with his arms folded on a railing. A corral, he thought. We've got a real corral. Just like in the cowboy TV shows. How am I going to get them to buy me a horse?

Behind him, perched motionless on the branches of a dead cedar, several crows were etched against the orange green sky, like black holes that led to a darkness beyond.

2

*T*he next morning, Christine hardly knew where to begin. The kitchen, she thought. I've got to clean the kitchen. I will not be overwhelmed. I will cope. I will cope overwhelmingly. I think.

She was alone. Joey was exploring with a reluctant Sleazy, and Nick had gone to the restaurant early. When you worked for Loreto Marino you went to work early. Nick's father came from the old school before the old school. For twenty years he and his wife had managed, then owned, a small restaurant on Manhattan's East Fourteenth Street. Loreto Marino had saved his money. Last year he had bought a large, waterfront restaurant on the North Shore. At the same time he had given Nick and Christine the down payment on their new home. "It's an investment," he had said. "I want my oldest son near the restaurant. He's a solid boy, my Nicky. The women love him. The men love him. It's an investment, I'm telling you. Take it, take it. I'll raise the prices on the veal." Christine knew him like a book. Exterior hardness, interior love. Just like Nick.

By three o'clock she had just started to make some headway when Joey burst through the door. In his hand was a large animal skull. "Hey, Mom," he said, "look at this. I found it in the woods down by the corral."

Christine stared at the gaping jaws and sharp, white teeth held up to her by her son. Her mouth turned down in quick revulsion. She could hardly bear to look at the thing. It was stark, savage, frightening. It stirred hidden nightmares within her, forgotten dreams, old terrors. After her initial shock, she tried to compose her face. She managed a smile but the remnants of the sudden fear remained in her eyes. She forced herself to touch it. "It looks like it might have been a dog, Joey. Maybe a collie or a Doberman."

"There are more of them down there, Mom."

"More?" Christine looked puzzled.

"Yeah, there's lots of them. All different kinds. Can I bring some of them up to my room?"

"I think one of these things is quite enough." Christine stood up. She felt a vague apprehension as her eyes followed her son trotting off to his room with his new possession. She clasped her arms around herself tightly and shuddered involuntarily. Shaking her head she returned to her unpacking.

As Christine carefully unwrapped her paints, brushes, and easel, she saw a faded charcoal sketch of Nick's face at the bottom of the carton. She smiled. She remembered when she had made it. Ten years ago. At the Metropolitan Museum of Art. She had been sketching a Renoir. She had noticed this incredibly handsome man seated in front of a Van Gogh, staring at it fiercely. She had gone to lunch in the museum restaurant. When she returned, the man was still there. He doesn't belong here, Christine had thought. Although good-looking, his face was too hard, too streetwise. More the face of a hoodlum than an art lover. Was he, perhaps, planning to steal it? She had begun her sketching again. Another hour had passed. When Christine looked down she was amazed to find that she had made a sketch of the hoodlum's face, Renoir forgotten. The man had not looked at her, yet Christine was positive that he was aware of her presence. When he got up to leave, Christine had felt a panic. She had not known why. At the room's entrance he turned and looked at her. A door opened and then quietly closed within Christine. She gathered her things together and walked with him out of the museum. They walked down Fifth Avenue in the warm spring air. They did not talk. Three months later, they were married.

Nick drove into the circular driveway at six o'clock. He found Christine in the bedroom, arranging her hair.

He walked to her and kissed the back of her neck lingeringly.

"Neck man," Christine said and tapped him with her brush.

"Also a leg man, an ass man, and a breast man. And now, a very excited man. Let's not go tonight."

Christine shook her head. "My father *warned* me about anyone not born in Connecticut. Nick, we have to go. We have to," she made quotation signs with her fingers, "'meet the neighbors.'"

"Well, then let's come home early," he suggested, bending to nibble her left earlobe.

Christine's eyes closed. "You are incredible. How early?"

"Very early. Especially if they're all like that Drogin character. Say, who is this Anderson guy, anyway?"

"I haven't the vaguest. Apparently he's our nearest neighbor. I think it was very nice of him to invite us, sight unseen, as it were."

"Not so, my cabbage. He saw us last night when we were walking Sleazy. Great big guy standing on his lawn with a little old lady next to him."

"His mother?"

"Who knows. After meeting Drogin I'd say it was most probably his girl friend. These people are weird out here."

Nick heard Christine laugh as he turned to the mirror and buttoned his shirt. He stared at the reflection of his face. Don't do it, Nicholas, he warned himself. Don't start putting these people down. You're going to be living with them for a long time. Anderson will turn out to be an okay guy. Looks like he used to play football.

Since Nick had known Christine, he had begun to experience some emotions that were new to him. Tough streetboy Nick Marino, king of the East Village, had felt, for the first time in his life, rough, unpolished, inadequate in certain indefinable ways. It rarely happened when he was alone with Christine. But whenever they were with Christine's various circles of friends; at her parents' country club in Connecticut; with the opera and art crowd in Manhattan; at the dozens of cocktail parties they had attended, he had noticed it. He did not like the feeling. There was something about these people, an impalpable, cerebral snobbery, that he could not fight, that brought a defensive scowl to his lips. It also made him intensely jealous about Christine. He still thought of himself as a barbaric, dark intruder who had entered some bright, sophisticate kingdom, stolen a princess, and who now had to be constantly on guard against her rescue by some intellectual prince from Harvard or Yale.

Nick adjusted his tie in the mirror. Cool it, man, he told himself. Shake off those tired old ghosts. Leave your host and his friends alone. All lovely people, I'm sure. And no one's going to carry your wife away. Not with old Nicky boy around, they're not.

"I better go help Joey with his tie," he said.

Christine turned toward him. "Nick," she said, "you never really told me why you were staring at that Van Gogh for so long."

"At who?"

"The Van Gogh. At the museum that day."

"You've asked me that before, my love."

"I'm asking again."

After a moment, Nick said, "I was trying to make up my mind, my prying sweet, whether it was worth all his mad torment, to paint like that."

"And what did you decide?"

"Don't rush me," Nick said. He waved his finger at Christine and then left the room.

As they walked away from the house, Christine looked back. "We'd better leave Sleazy here," she said. "He had a run-in with a chipmunk today and lost. If he sees all those people at the Andersons' he'll pass out." The dog tried to follow them but a reprimand from Nick halted him in his tracks. He stood there quivering, his thin tail between his frail legs.

Nick shook his head. "God, that's pitiful," he said.

"I love him, Dad," Joey protested stoutly.

Nick stopped and knelt down in front of Joey. "I do, too, son. It was just another one of Daddy's silly jokes." He looked steadily into the boy's eyes and gently straightened the half-sized tie. "Say kiddo, who's the best dad in the whole world?"

"You are, Dad," Joey said, playing their familiar game. "And who's the best kid in the whole world?"

"You are, pally. You are." After a brief moment, Nick rose to his feet.

Christine put her arm around Nick's waist, her eyes on the ground in front of her. She had seen that look before. She was jealous of the unbounded love that

Nick had for his son and at the same time she adored him for it.

The Anderson home was located several hundred yards from their house, near the end of the narrow cove that was Mill Harbor. The path that led them along the shore was overgrown on the inland side by twelve-foot rushes interspersed with tall purple flowers, wild tiger lilies, and young weeping willows rippling in the June breeze. Behind the rushes, gnarled cedars and ageless oaks loomed up into the evening sky. On their right, the waters of the inlet sighed secretly against the sea grass. The mast of a lone sailboat, sunset-tipped, rocked gently from side to side. The silence was a presence, the air humid and tidal.

They passed the Anderson boathouse, huge, un-used, its cavernous entrance yawning toward the water. A rusted rail line led out of it down through the grass to the water, twisted and covered with seaweed. The windows were boarded up, shattered glass was everywhere. Its dull yellow paint was cracked and flaking. Christine grasped Joey's hand. She did not know why.

As they passed the boathouse, they looked across a large, uncut lawn toward the Anderson home. The first impression was that it went on forever, meandering in disconnected additions deep into the encroaching vege-tation. It was five stories in height, the disarrayed wooden roof shingles rising above the tallest of the pine trees that surrounded it. The magnificent work-manship on the aging house was apparent even at that distance, but everything seemed to be sagging, crumbling, giving it an aura of time forgotten, corrupt enchantment. Nick and Christine could not take their eyes from it as they walked through the tall grass toward the sound of voices.

"There they are!" A small, well-dressed woman waved at them from the crowd of people gathered on the patio. "My God!" she said. "They're beautiful!" She was carefully made-up, used her hands when she spoke, and had a superior figure. "Welcome to the land of sophistication and money." She took Christine's hand. "I'm Kimberly Potts. This is my husband, George." The woman waved at a short, bald man to her right. Christine got a quick impression of a thin, immaculately clipped moustache, small feet, and perfect tailoring.

"Welcome to the land of taxes," George Potts said. "Good to have you aboard." Nick introduced Joey, who shook Potts's hand shyly. "Nice to make your acquaintance. You certainly are a handsome young man. As a matter of fact, Marinos, Kim is right, you *are* a good-looking family. What a relief. All we've had to look at for the past few years are Anderson and Drogin. It's nice to see some decent-looking people for a change."

"Ah, George," Maynard Drogin's gaunt figure loomed up beside Potts. "I've asked you never to mention my name when you're drunk. You know how you tend to slur your words."

Potts squinted up at his neighbor. "Maynard, this is

a social occasion. Why do you look like you've just fallen off your horse?"

"Because I've just fallen off my horse." As Drogin turned toward Christine, she suppressed a quick smile. "It is charming to meet you again, Mrs. Marino. I'm sorry you had to meet Mill Harbor's worst element so soon." He pointed a long finger at Potts. "There really should be some sort of zoning law for persons of his ilk. Has he told you how rich he is yet?"

"No," Christine laughed, "not yet."

"He will. It would be disgusting if it weren't so boring."

Potts was looking with distaste at the tall man. "An ascot and boots! Ye gods, Maynard, that went out in 1927."

"Be careful these boots don't step on your tiny Guccis and make you whimper. Dear people, I must get a drink. This man makes my mouth parch with unspoken vulgarities."

Kimberly Potts shook her head. "So much for the two perpetual adolescents." She put her arm around Christine's waist. "Let me introduce you folks to some of your new neighbors."

As they walked across the crumbling patio, shaking hands, making small conversation, Christine watched Nick through her long eyelashes. She knew his aversion to people who were not his New York City crowd, but tonight he looked almost at ease. She noticed, with some reluctance, how the women reacted to his dark, good looks. The social acceptance of women had never been a problem for Nick. Nick's problem was Nick. Christine called it his Hell's Kitchen syndrome, resentment of the necessary social graces, the intellectual amenities, or, as Nick phrased it, the bullshit.

Christine had mingled with people like these all her life. She had tried but could not understand Nick's attitude. She liked these people, was a part of them. Smooth, successful people, people with a well-groomed gleam about them, who always smelled appropriately expensive. It was Westport all over again: her father's numerous legal partners, her mother's PTA-tennis group. She was comfortable with them because she knew them, they held no surprises. Nick was different. Nick was the city. Tough. Unpredictable.

Kimberly Potts stopped in front of a tall, nautically dressed man who held a pipe in one hand and a drink in the other. "And this," she said, "is our resident genius. Terrible sailor, eligible bachelor, the eminent Dr. Bowen Stirner. He teaches anthropology at Hofstra University and is famous throughout the Eastern Seaboard for his wit and charm, he tells me."

Christine looked up at the tanned, handsome face, the slightly bent nose, the tightly curled blond hair. The gray eyes lingered on her for several moments before moving to Nick and Joey.

"I'm sure if you hear 'welcome aboard' one more time you will hemorrhage," Stirner said, smiling, "so may I merely say 'welcome to Mill Harbor and all its false and transient pleasures.'"

As Christine shook Stirner's hand, she saw something move behind his steady, musing gaze and when he turned to greet some other guests she knew with the surety of a beautiful woman that she had touched him somehow, that in the eye of his mind he was still looking down into her face. She had grown accustomed to the admiration of men, but this had been different, something swift and deep that Stirner had tried, with little success, to hide. She glanced at Nick. Christine had made peace with her attractiveness to men long ago. Nick never had. His quick, flaring jealousy had often been a source of anguish for both of them. Nick's face showed nothing. Impulsively, she clasped his arm tightly with both of her hands.

With the intuition of the totally jealous, Nick's glance rose to follow Stirner through the crowd the moment he felt the pressure of Christine's grasp. His eyes did not move when Kimberly Potts began speaking again.

"That man," she said. "That man. It ought to be illegal to look like that and be so absolutely brilliant. He has a seven thousand IQ, or something. He's really a genius."

"Ah," Nick said.

"The women are all mad for him, except for myself, of course. George is really so cute, and besides he *does* have all that money. But that Bowen, he's just so absolutely . . . charming, don't you think?"

"Yes," Nick said. "Oh, yes. Definitely." Christine glanced up at Nick quickly. She did not like the tone of his voice. "Let me see," Nick continued. "I'll bet he graduated from Yale. Or was it Harvard?"

"I think it was Princeton, actually. Summa cum laude. Incredible honors and all that."

"Imagine," Nick said. "Summa cum laude. My goodness." He was staring at Stirner's back. Christine saw that Nick's eyes had hardened perceptibly. It was Joey who broke the hidden tension.

"Hey, Dad," he said. "Look, they've got a swimming pool. Can we go over and see it?"

Nick's face softened immediately. "Why sure, pally. Ladies, will you excuse us men for just a moment?"

Soon after they left, Kimberly Potts excused herself to join her husband. As she waited for Nick, Christine's casual glance roamed over the huge, tree-shrouded house. High in a fourth-story window she caught the movement of a curtain being pulled back. Peering upward curiously, she saw an old woman standing behind the dusty panes staring down at the people below. From what Christine could see, her features were frail, her long white hair tied into a bun at the back of her head. She seemed to be looking intently at someone in the crowd below her. In another moment she was gone.

"Ah, I see you've met my mother. She is not a party person, I'm afraid."

Christine turned toward the deep voice behind her. There, expensively tailored in a gray suit and gray accessories was the largest man she had ever seen. It was not a pleasant physique. The huge shoulders sloped from an unbelievably thick neck, the bulk of the body was arresting, an affront. Two rows of small, even teeth smiled at her from a large, wide face. The full head of platinum hair was sleeked back along the temples. The face could have been handsome but it was not. The features had a raw, glistening, swollen look. The icy, pale blue eyes were devouring her with a surprised voraciousness.

Oh, my God, Christine thought, it's Odin. Never had she conceived of anyone looking so Nordic, so far beyond Teutonic.

"My dear Mrs. Marino," Odin said. "I am Karl Anderson, your host and neighbor." One huge hand offered her a drink, the other swept past Christine's outstretched arm and rested on her stomach. Slowly, insolently, it moved down until his fingers outlined her crotch and then were gone. "Welcome to Paradise," he said.

White, electric shock flooded through Christine. The grossness of what he had done, shielded from the others by his broad back, filled her with a paralyzing rage. She stood motionless, her eyes locked into the mocking blue gaze of the huge man before her. In delayed reaction, she threw her drink into his face.

The smile never changed. "I have heard," he said, dabbing at his face with a handkerchief, "that hatred is not far removed from love. What a superb beginning we have made." With a slight bow of his head, he turned and walked away.

Trembling, Christine closed her eyes. Why, she thought, oh, why does there always have to be one son of a bitch? Just once I'd like to go some place where there was not a single lecherous son of a bitch.

"Try not to sleep standing up." It was Nick beside her. He handed her a drink. "Our neighbors will think they're boring us."

With effort, Christine adjusted her face. "I haven't been bored," she said. She drained her glass halfway down.

"I see you've met the Viking," Nick said, nodding in Anderson's direction. "I could have used a guy that size in my old neighborhood."

"He's an old dear," Christine answered. She finished her drink.

"Hey," Nick said. "Slow down." He looked at her carefully. "Anything the matter, pal o' mine?"

Christine looked into those smoldering brown eyes that always seemed on the verge of bursting into flame. She had a vision of Nick and their host rolling around the lawn locked in mortal combat. She had seen Nick in a fight once. Outside of his father's restaurant on Fourteenth Street. The man had been larger than Nick, like Anderson, but it had been no contest. Nick had grown up using his fists, and he knew all the tricks. He fought like a machine, unstoppable, almost disinterested. It had frightened Christine at the time.

"Everything's just fine, *amore*." She managed a smile. "Let's take Joey and eat. He must be starved."

While they ate, Christine's eyes followed Anderson coldly. I can stand you, neighbor, she thought. I can stand even you. I love my house, my lawn, my trees. I love my kid, my handsome, jealous husband, my cowardly dog. And screw you, neighbor Anderson!

The old woman Christine had seen behind the window curtain appeared at the door to the patio. She was even frailer than Christine had thought. There was a shawl draped around her shoulders. A prototype grandmother, Christine thought. She's perfect. All grandmothers should look like that.

"Mother," Anderson said loudly. "What a surprise. The last time my mother came to a party, Hoover was president. What brings you out into the dark of night, my precious?"

The old woman looked at him oddly, almost conspiratorily. "Introduce me to our guests, Karl," she said, taking his arm. Her voice was surprisingly strong.

When the Andersons came to Christine, she shook the old woman's thin hand warmly. "So nice to meet you," she said.

Her words were not heard. Mrs. Anderson was staring at Nick with rapt intensity. When he shook her hand, she took hold of his arm, her eyes never leaving his face.

"Another conquest for surface charm," Christine said to Nick over the rim of her glass.

"Mature perceptions are invariably sensitive," Nick answered. He smiled and waved his fingers at her as he led the clinging old woman to a chair.

In front of her, Karl Anderson was watching the two of them, a slow smile spreading across his face. Christine turned quickly and joined a group of people at the far end of the patio.

"We were just talking about your house," Kimberly Potts informed her. "George says it must be haunted or something. There have been three different families living there since we moved here seven years ago. How many times have you sold it, Maynard?"

"Twice," Drogin replied. "I sold it to the Levines, who sold it to you folks."

"I knew the Levines very well," Bowen Stirner added through his pipe smoke. "Nice couple. They loved it here, but they left when their daughter went a little, you know." He tapped his forehead with his finger.

"Oh?" Christine said. "Do you know what happened?"

"They never really told me. One day they were just *gone*. No farewells. Nothing. They've never been back."

"Cut it out, Bowen," George Potts said. "You'll scare our new neighbors. Bad for real estate values."

"Real estate values have never been better," Maynard Drogin commented. "The last bad thing that happened in Mill Harbor was eight years ago. The tooth fairy forgot to leave George a quarter."

"That's more than the fairies leave you every Friday night," Potts retorted. "Now that you've said the eff word, Maynard, why not get it all out. It will be therapeutic."

"I do not argue with bedwetters," Drogin said, winking at Christine.

Christine shook her head. "Why would anybody leave so quickly? They must have spoken to some of you, given some sort of reason."

Kimberly Potts looked at Christine's troubled face. "Now I want all of you to stop this silly talk, right now. Haunted houses! Really! I'd rather hear George and Maynard try to be funny." She put her arm around Christine.

As the conversations dwindled down, Christine looked over at Nick. He was still talking to Mrs. Anderson. The old woman was clinging to his arm, drinking in his features while he spoke. The icy Anderson eyes followed his lips, roamed his face in rapt concentration. We *are* an attractive couple, Christine thought. There's no getting away from it.

The farewells began. They were long and cordial, with many affirmations of future meetings. Although his face was relaxed and casual, Bowen Stirner pressed Christine's hand good-bye. Christine smiled a polite, automatic smile. I ought to have a cigarette after that handshake, she thought. Yes, you've got it all, professor. The looks, the magnetism, lovely tan, lovely. But this is Christine Marino. This is Nick's girl. So good night, good doctor, and pleasant dreams. She walked past Karl Anderson's outstretched hand, her mouth tensing, her eyes looking straight ahead. Nick disengaged Mrs. Anderson with difficulty. As he walked away the old woman stared after him strangely.

They did not go directly home, but walked toward the end of the inlet along the shoreline path. Beyond the inlet and the slim peninsula to their right, the lights of Connecticut glimmered, a small electric galaxy. In front of them the old mill loomed squarely in the moonlight. As Joey ran in front of them, they kissed. They discussed their neighbors.

"Dr. Eminent Eligible was looking at you like a falcon circling a titmouse," Nick said.

"I confess it," Christine said, "although I'm not crazy about your simile. You didn't do so badly yourself. Oh, a little old, a little quaint, but definitely hypnotized."

Nick's arms circled her waist like a caress. "Score two for the Magnificent Marinos," he said.

When they came to the end of Mill Harbor, they turned around and walked toward home through the warm, quiet night. As they crossed the corral, it was Christine who saw it first.

"Oh, my God," she gasped, her hands clutching the sides of her head. Nick tried, too late, to turn Joey around. There in the grass in front of them was the head of Sleazy. It looked as if it had been torn from his body, the dead eyes burst from their sockets, the teeth gaping in frozen agony.

3

As Christine drove toward the Mill Harbor police station the next morning, her eyes were red, her mouth a straight, tight line. Every time she glanced at the box on the seat beside her, the car lurched forward with her impatience. Nick, on his only morning off, had wanted to stay home with Joey who, in his young anger and bewilderment, had refused to come out of his room that morning. Christine had volunteered to go to the police. She parked the car and strode up the station steps, the grisly package under her arm.

"I'd like to talk to someone in connection with a

murder," she said to the police sergeant at the desk.

The sergeant looked at her steadily. "You can give your information to Lieutenant Broderick, ma'am." He took her name and address and brought it to a slim, well-dressed man standing at a desk behind him. The lieutenant noted her name and indicated a chair beside his desk. The calm, green eyes had a hardness within. "Did you say 'murder,' Mrs. Marino?"

"Yes," Christine said. "My dog was murdered last night."

The lieutenant nodded. His expression did not change. He typed the information Christine gave him, looked soberly at the contents of the box for a long time, and then sat down and stared at it, his finger stroking his bright red moustache.

"I want this maniac caught and put in jail," Christine demanded in a low, angry voice. "He came on our property. He did a thing like this." She pointed toward the box. "I want you to catch this crazy bastard, Lieutenant, and put him away."

Lieutenant Broderick stared moodily at her legs for several moments. "You bought the Levine house on Kensington Road?" he asked finally.

"Yes," she replied impatiently. "What are you going to do about this?" Again she pointed to the box.

"Mrs. Marino, this is not the first case like this we've had in the area. In the past several years there have been twenty to thirty complaints of this nature. Pets disappear, get mutilated. Sometimes . . ."

"Sometimes what?" Christine asked, her voice not as firm as she would have liked it to be.

"I'm not at liberty to discuss details with you, Mrs. Marino. We have been working on this and will continue to do so, please be assured of that."

Christine's anger was turning into anxiety. "Why did you ask me if I had bought the Levine house?"

"Well, they . . . had some pet trouble, too, just before they left." The detective stood up. "I'll keep you informed, Mrs. Marino."

Christine looked up at him. "What kind of pet trouble?"

Lieutenant Broderick shook his head slightly. "We'll keep this box for pathology. I'll be in touch with you as soon as anything develops. Good-bye, Mrs. Marino."

As Christine drove away to do her food shopping, unanswered questions, elements of fear, darted about in her thoughts. Try as she did to put them out of her mind, they persisted.

Nick Marino walked out of the house into the bright sunlight. Christine had gone to the police station and Joey refused to come out of his room. He surveyed the extensive lawn in front of him and sighed audibly. This place will revert to the jungle, he thought, if I don't get that slave driver father of mine to give me more than one day off a week. He walked to a toolshed at the back of the house and found an old hand mower behind a pile of garden hose. He took it out onto the lawn, and started to oil it. Here I go, he thought. Harry Homebody. The boys on Twelfth Street should see me now. He laughed out loud.

As Nick stood up wiping the oil from his hands, the

strummed notes of a guitar reached his ears. He looked toward the trees beyond the corral. The music had no particular melody but had a soft beauty that pleased him. Then the first sweet notes of a woman's voice lilted in the bright air. Nick listened. The wordless song flowed around him, clear and pure. Without exactly knowing why, he began to walk toward the trees, leaving the mower slanting upward toward the sun. As he entered the cool shade of the pines, he changed his direction, thrusting the impeding branches roughly away.

The singer was sitting on a rock ten yards in front of him. As Nick came into the small clearing, the music stopped. She looked up at him, her head slightly to one side. "Lose your golf ball?" she asked pleasantly.

Nick tried to gather his thoughts. The girl was beautiful. There was not an imperfection in face or body. Her long blond hair hung down to the pants of her bikini bathing suit. "Great Caesar," Nick said. Terrible. He tried again. "Where did you learn to sing like that?"

"Never answer a question with a question." The girl seemed somehow mildly amused.

Nick gathered himself together as much as he could. "I'm Nick Marino. I live in that house over there. I cut lawns. Who are you, little girl?"

"I'm Karla Anderson, Nick Marino. Home from Europe. A sociology major. Three point four average. One hundred and fifteen pounds. Blond. I'm your neighbor."

Nick nodded his head in open admiration. "Hello,

neighbor." After a long pause he said, "You're Karl Anderson's daughter?"

"Yes. Don't look so surprised. My father is not pretty nor is he lovable. I am both." Then, as an afterthought, "My mother was a truly beautiful woman. She died in an auto accident when I was very young."

"I'm sorry," Nick said. "Miss Anderson, I don't know how to break this to you, but I think your grandmother is in love with me."

The blue eyes glittered. "Really?" Her stare was intense now. "Why then, Nicholas, you must be a devil with women." Her face had become serious, masked.

"No devil here," Nick said. "Just your ordinary, happily married, lustful mortal."

The girl's eyes flared slightly. "How lustful *are* you, Nicholas?"

Nick scuffed his foot. "Shucks, ma'am," he said.

"And your marriage vows, Nicholas. Do you keep them all? Are you, let's say, obedient?"

Nick appraised her coolly. "Say," he said, "you're some piece of work, Lolita."

"Answer my question."

"Of course. I am loyal, honorable, faithful . . ."

"And lustful." The smile came back to her face. "The lustful Mr. Marino." Her raised knee moved languidly from side to side.

Nick looked at her thoughtfully. "I think I'll go home now," he said.

As he walked away, the girl resumed her singing. Nick's steps became smaller, his pace slower. By the time he reached the corral he was almost walking in place. He stopped and turned. He closed his eyes. The song drifted through the air like a fragrance.

Christine did not get home until after one o'clock. Nick was not in the house and Joey had decided to come down to the living room to watch television, his handsome face still sad and swollen from crying. Annoyed at Nick for leaving Joey alone, she made him a quick lunch and went upstairs to continue the unpacking.

Nick did not come home until almost six o'clock.

"Where have you been?" Christine called from the kitchen. "You left Joey alone. I made lunch for you . . ." Nick appeared at the kitchen door. If Christine hadn't known better, she would have sworn he was drunk.

"I've been," he explained, "inspecting the north forty." Imitation of W. C. Fields. "Ah, yes, the old north forty."

"You great city idiot. You have a tough time opening up a can of corn. Some farmer. There's only one thing you can raise successfully."

"Thank you, fans. Listen, if I told you I spent the whole afternoon mesmerized in the clutches of a young, blond nymphomaniac, what would you say?"

"I'd say you were very, very lucky. As it is, you're just very, very crazy."

Nick walked over and kissed her hard. He seemed unsteady on his feet, his eyes looked dazed, distracted. "I must be crazy," he said. "I don't know, I . . . What the hell . . . What the hell."

Christine looked at him closely. "What is it, honey?" she said.

Nick shook his head and shrugged his shoulders. "I'm late for work. I'll eat at the restaurant." He pulled himself away and walked quickly out of the room. Christine watched his retreating back for a moment, frowning in puzzlement. Then she shrugged her shoulders and called Joey down to dinner.

As Christine ate, she watched Joey's sad face, his downcast eyes. He was poking listlessly at his food.

"Joey, what is it, honey? You haven't eaten anything. Is it Sleazy?"

Joey nodded his head without looking up.

"Honey, the detective will find whoever or whatever did that to Sleazy. You can be sure of that."

Joey nodded. He still did not look up at her. Tears had begun to form in the corners of his eyes.

Christine's heart melted. "Sweetheart, sometimes things happen to us that we don't understand, that are hard to take. We have to learn . . ."

The wet eyes flared up at her. Christine saw the Marino hardness etched in the small face. "He was my *friend*, Ma. Why would anybody do that to him? He was *my* dog, and somebody . . ." He slid from the table and ran up the stairs.

Christine heard the door slam. She stared sadly at his empty chair. An idea had been forming in her mind ever since her talk with Lieutenant Broderick. She had disregarded it as a little hysterical but as she sat there remembering Joey's face she decided to follow through with it before going up to comfort her son. She looked in her personal telephone directory and found Gloria Levine's number. The former owners had moved to Connecticut before Christine had even seen the house, but she had met them at the contract signing.

"Hello?" The voice was Mrs. Levine's. Quiet, without intonation, just as Christine remembered.

"Hi, Mrs. Levine. This is Christine Marino."

"Yes?"

"Yes. Yes, it is." Christine was taken aback by the lack of friendliness.

"What's the matter?" She spoke in a tired monotone.

"Why, nothing really. Well, that's not quite true. It seems that our dog was killed last night."

There was silence on the other end.

"And I, well, was wondering whether you'd ever had any trouble like that when you lived here. I mean, say, with pets or anything."

Again there was no response.

"I, um, was talking to the police about it today, and a detective said you had some pet trouble a while back yourselves. And I, uh, was wondering whether there was anything to it. Whether there had been some trouble of any kind."

"Some trouble?" Mrs. Levine's voice was low, stretched thin. "Yes, we had some trouble. My daughter spent five months in a mental institution because we had some trouble."

Christine's heart jumped. "Oh, I'm so sorry. Could you tell me what . . ."

There was a soft click on the other end and the line went dead.

Christine sat staring at the telephone for a long time. She stood up and went to a tall living room window. A wind was blowing across the tops of the trees, showing the silver undersides of the leaves in the moonlight. A few clouds flew swiftly across the sky. She hugged herself tightly as she gazed at the dark, rustling woods beyond the corral.

I don't like this, she thought. I don't like this at all. She walked upstairs and knocked on Joey's door.

4

The next few days passed uneventfully and, and in the happiness of her new home, Christine forgot the fears that had begun to nag her. Joey was still a problem until the Saturday morning when Nick drove up and told them mysteriously to look in the station wagon. There, sitting in the back seat, was the biggest, blackest, roughest-looking Great Dane that Christine had ever seen. Although she wished that Nick had discussed it with her, the look on Joey's face decided everything.

"Hey, Dad!" Joey's face was flushed with joy. "He's the toughest. Can we keep him? Is he mine?"

"Yup. Yup," Nick said, looking at Christine for approval.

Christine shook her head but she could not help smiling. "You rat," she said under her breath. "You might have told me." Nick took the Great Dane from the car and he and Joey held on to the leash that restrained the lunging dog.

"He's so strong!" Joey said in wonderment.

"He's outrageous," Nick said. "He's a trained guard dog. He's a watchdog. I think he even knows karate. His name's Attila."

Christine and Joey laughed. Looking at Joey's face, Christine knew that Sleazy was finally forgotten. She linked arms with Nick. "Sometimes you're a very clever daddy," she said.

"And a very clever lover?" He nuzzled her ear.

"Sometimes," she said. Christine looked up at Nick as he watched his son's eager face. She put her arm around his shoulder and snuggled close to him.

She waited until after lunch to break the news to Nick. "Honey," she said, pouring him more coffee, "it's Henrietta time."

"Oh, no!" Nick rolled his eyes and slapped his forehead. "We just got rid . . . had the pleasure of her company a few months ago."

"It's been over a year, Nick, and Cousin Jody says she will permanently maim her if she stays another day. She's taken up French cooking. The last thing she cooked was Jody's stove."

"She cooked the stove?"

"She passed out with a rack of lamb in the oven."

Henrietta Knapp was Christine's unwanted, alcoholic aunt. Since she had no home of her own, Christine's family passed her around periodically like some untidy family heirloom, loved but unwanted.

"Chris, we just moved in. Is it absolutely necessary?"

"Please, Nick. It's just for three months. Until Albert gets home from Europe. He adores her." Her eyes had that pleading look Nick could never refuse.

Aunt Henrietta arrived two days later. One small valise and a large canvas tote bag that clinked suspiciously. Joey, who was fascinated by his great aunt, ran to hug her while Nick paid the taxi. "Watch the wig, sweetie," she said. She hugged Joey for a long moment and then adjusted her hair. She held her glasses up, tied around her neck by nylon fishing line, and peered at Christine. "Not enough makeup and you're much too thin" was her verdict.

The dinner that night was a loud and happy one. Christine had outdone herself and Nick opened up his best bottle of wine. He complained about Henrietta, but he enjoyed her company. Henrietta was a marvel to him. He had never seen her drunk, but he had rarely seen her sober either. She maintained a continuous alcoholic equilibrium that only the experienced eye could detect.

"Sure I drink a little," she said to Nick and Christine as she adjusted a cigarette into a long, metal holder. "Listen, I'm sixty-seven years old. I'm short, fat, and my skin is gone. I am lacking teeth, half of my hair, a major portion of my small intestine, and any sort of talent. I suffer from flatulence, receding gums, inferior breath, varicose veins, sagging you-know-whats"—she glanced at Joey—"myopia, and nicotine addiction. Two of my toes have crossed over. I have few friends. I live in a valise, and am prone to diarrhea. Now, if you were me, wouldn't you drink?"

"Yes," Nick and Christine said in unison.

Henrietta lit her cigarette and smiled. "I have, however, one thing that drives men crazy," she said.

"What?" Nick said in mock disbelief.

She exhaled slowly. "I give in easily."

Christine squealed with laughter and went over and impulsively threw her arms around her aunt. "You're too much," she said.

With Henrietta there to watch Joey, Christine had more time to devote to herself. She put her house in some sort of order; she walked down to the water and painted, the breeze blowing through her hair; she sunbathed; she swam. A week passed in this fashion before Lieutenant Broderick appeared at the door.

"Just checking, Mrs. Marino. Have there been any further . . . incidents since I spoke to you?"

"No," Christine answered, "and there won't be any more incidents around here." She pointed over his shoulder to the Great Dane standing behind him in the driveway, his eyes watching alertly, his body tensed. "Meet Attila, Lieutenant. I'd like to see that maniac or whatever-it-is fool with *him*."

Lieutenant Broderick looked at the dog thoughtfully. "Good idea," he said.

"Come in and have a cup of coffee, Lieutenant. I want to ask you something."

The slim man looked at his watch. "I can give you five minutes of valuable police time before I take my nap in the car," he replied.

Christine introduced Henrietta, who eyed the officer quizzically. She poured him a cup of coffee and sat down in front of him.

"You know what I'm going to ask," she began.

"Yes, I do. Is it necessary?" He glanced at Henrietta.

"Yes, it is. I want to know what happened to my dog."

"It was just like all the others, Mrs. Marino. Somebody twisted his head off. It's as simple and nasty as that."

A sudden, silent shriek tore through Christine.

"You asked me, Mrs. Marino." The lieutenant was looking down at his coffee cup.

Henrietta stared at them both unbelievingly. "That nice little dog you had, honey? Somebody around here . . . did that?"

Lieutenant Broderick rose to his feet. "We're doing what we can on it, Mrs. Marino. We'll get him. Meanwhile, I'm glad you have that dog out there. He's a champ." Christine saw him to the door, still shaken. He looked down at her, then touched her shoulder. "We will get him, Mrs. Marino. Most probably some nut who hates animals."

Henrietta had followed them to the door, squinting through her cigarette smoke. "I hope, dearie, that he likes people," she said quietly.

5

From the diary of Henrietta Knapp:

July 1.

Settled in enfin. *Lovely house. How I love these three. A marriage made* au ciel. *Joey looks just like his gorgeous father. Christine like an angel. She has that certain quality we Knapps have. An ethereal* je ne sais quoi. *I can still see it in parts of my forehead, the upsweep of my chins, although everything else seems to have fallen considerably.* Le temps, le temps, toujours le temps. *If only my face could stop the clocks of time.* Mais non, *one cannot, one must not.*

A Dr. Stirner called while Christine was out. Nice voice. Charmant *but mysterious. Wanted to take Chris-*

tine and Joey sailing. Offered to include me. What does one wear? *Wig blow off? Mal de mer pills? A hundred distractions.*

A truly disciplined Chablis at dinner tonight. Improperly chilled but with an aroma one could not forget. Or remember. Très piquant, très . . . *funky.*

July 2.

Morning aperitif a true delight. Some unsung rosé from New York State, I believe. A surly little grape which somehow manages to be amusing without trying. I think the prune juice affected its clarity, but age has its necessities and petit *dissatisfactions. Ah,* la vie vieille.

Took Joey clamming this morning. Don't like him to be alone after that nasty dog incident. Very few clams but found an old umbrella I shall renovate.

1:00 P.M. Dr. Stirner drove by. Christine and Joey out buying soccer shoes. Quelle catastrophe! *Opened the door in a state of* habiller incroyable. *Insisted on taking us out on his sailboat. Christine told me she won't go with him. Personally, I would sail with that man to Havana. On a hollowed-out log.*

Continue this entry after daiquiris and lunch.

Glorious afternoon! Glorious clouds chasing each other across an azure sky for my entertainment. Birds everywhere: winging, singing, laying. The too bright sun looks down on all, thinking what fools we mortals be, myself not included, except for those few weeks in Atlantic City. All Nature is tranquil because the universe, as we know it, is one.

My problem: how to get more ice without getting up.

July 3.

Moody tonight. Warm beer always brings on La Tristesse de la Nuit. *Tears of retrospection. Look at that mascara. Cruel mirror, mirror without a heart. With this wig I look like Shirley Temple playing Dracula. Shirley Temple, Jane Withers, Bobby Breen. Where do the years go? What is Life? Why are we here? Where is Love? Where are my shoes?*

To complete my day, found something in the bottom of the tequila bottle tonight I can't even discuss! *I mean, why me? Why not someone else?*

Good-bye tequila, bonjour tristesse.

6

Christine sat in front of her dressing table mirror applying her eye makeup carefully. When she was done, she paused and looked at herself. "You're beautiful, kiddo, just beautiful," she said aloud.

It had been a week since Lieutenant Broderick's visit had reawakened those small, gnawing fears, but the happiness of her days had dispelled them. She loved her new house, the quiet afternoons of Mill Harbor, and Joey and Nick seemed to share her happiness.

She glanced at her watch. Nick had not returned

from his swim at the Andersons' pool yet. They were going to be late for Maynard Drogin's Fourth of July party. Christine was looking forward to seeing the inside of that stark old mill he lived in.

Nick came up the stairs a few minutes later, a towel over his shoulders, a preoccupied look on his face.

"Please hurry, honey, we're late already." Christine called after him as he went into the bathroom. He had not given her his usual kiss on the neck and somehow it bothered her.

"Right, right," Nick said absently.

"Hey, are you training for the Olympics or something, Nicky? What do you *do* over there for two hours?"

There was no answer. A few minutes later Christine glanced into her mirror and saw Nick standing in the bathroom doorway, electric razor in hand. He was staring at her coldly. Christine's eyes widened. She turned around but he was gone.

"Nick?"

"Yes, my endive."

I must have been mistaken, she thought. The lights. The mirror. "Everything okay?"

"Perfect, my parsley."

The mill that Maynard Drogin had converted into a home stood on a narrow isthmus of land at the end of Mill Harbor. A large saltwater pond that rose and fell with the tide formed the other boundary of his property. Christine and Nick stepped carefully across the narrow walk above the sluice gate that controlled the pond's flow and approached the mill. Its faded red hulk rose sharply into the sky from the solid cement base that formed a dam.

"This place *is* Drogin," Nick said. "Weird. Stark and weird."

The door swung open and Maynard Drogin greeted them. "The beautiful Marinos! How glad I am to see you. I've been looking at George Potts all evening and my stomach is heaving. Come in, come in."

The bottom floor of the mill was one large room which was already filled with people. Dr. Bowen Stirner sauntered over to them. On his arm was a pretty young woman in blue jeans and a peasant blouse. She wore frameless glasses and no makeup.

Shaking Stirner's hand once again, Christine was surprised to note that her eyelids fluttered slightly. The fierce good looks of the man, his obvious attraction to her, made her uncomfortable. Nick's greeting did not make her feel any better.

"Hello, genius," he said. His smile was controlled, careful.

Stirner looked at him calculatingly for a long moment. He decided to laugh. "$E = mc^2$. Energy equals something, something squared," he said. "Marinos, this is Ursala Hauser. She works with me at Hofstra, is very intense, and is after my chairman's job."

The young woman shook their hands. "It's just a matter of time," she said. "Very glad to meet you."

As the four of them stood together, Christine again had the feeling that no matter where Bowen Stirner's gaze went, he was looking at her, was aware of her presence. After several minutes of conversation, Christine noticed Nick looking around the room as though searching for someone.

"See anybody you like?" she asked.

"As a matter of fact, I do." Nick walked across the room and sat down next to someone seated on a long leather couch. It was Mrs. Anderson. He looked back and winked at Christine as the old lady linked arms with him. Christine made a wry face, tipped an imaginary hat to him and walked with Bowen Stirner and the girl toward the bar.

It was a mistake. Standing by the bar was Karl Anderson.

"Hello, Karl," Bowen Stirner said. "Where is your lovely daughter tonight?"

"At home with a sunburn, I'm afraid." The alien smile spread slowly across Anderson's face. "I've brought my mother instead."

Lovely daughter, Christine thought? I wonder why Nick hadn't mentioned her. He must see her when he goes swimming over there. Her thoughts were interrupted by Anderson's voice.

"Mrs. Marino," he said. "Once again your beauty dazzles the eyes. I shall never forget our first meeting. Imagine. Meeting only once, and yet I feel that I know you. So very well," he added insinuatingly.

Christine looked steadily into the bright, mocking eyes. "Bowen, would you two excuse us for a moment," she said.

Puzzled, Stirner looked from Christine to Anderson and back again. "Of course," he said.

Christine turned and faced the large man. "Look, neighbor," she said evenly. "I just wanted to tell you.

If you ever touch me again, even try to shake my hand, I'm going to ask my husband to beat the hell out of you."

Anderson turned his huge head to look at Nick. "I quiver," he said.

"He's got two brothers, and a father who could do it by himself," Christine said, a little desperately, she thought. The man scared her.

"I tremble," Anderson said. As Christine turned to go, Anderson spoke pleasantly. "Mrs. Marino, this is ridiculous. We are neighbors. Civilized, tax-paying neighbors. Let us learn to live together in harmony." His eyes lost their amused look. "We should love one another, you and I. We are already halfway there, Mrs. Marino. Or may I call you Christine?"

"No, I think not."

His smile returned. "May I call you tomorrow? You are looking at a lonely man, Christine. A widower, whose wife's untimely heart attack has left him bereft of female companionship in the very prime of life."

"You're drunk."

"Intoxicated by your presence, perhaps. You will learn to like me, Christine. Everybody in this community knows and likes Karl Anderson. I am a pillar. My name is a standard at Boy Scout meetings. I am an expert in the care of shrubs. How can you not like me?"

"You mean outside of your grossness and your arrogance?" Christine was surprised by her cruelty.

Something stirred deep within Anderson's eyes. "Ah. Beauty has its privileges." That terrible smile again. "You'll see. You'll learn. I grow on people."

"So do warts." Christine turned and walked away. It

had been a good exit line but she felt no victory. The man behind her was laughing.

Christine did not enjoy her dinner. Although the food was excellent, Karl Anderson had chosen to sit directly opposite her and his cold eyes seldom left her face. Next to him, Mrs. Anderson's eyes were glued to every movement that Nick made. She ate when he ate, even wiped her mouth when he did. Christine could not help smiling at her simple adoration. How could a sweet-looking woman like that have such a crude, boorish son, she wondered.

Karl Anderson had noticed that Nick was still looking around the room. He caught Nick's attention. With Nick coldly looking on, he looked under his plate and shook his head. He stirred around in his coffee, shook his head again, and smiled up at Nick. He lifted his napkin off his lap, stared at his groin and scratched his head puzzledly. The strange grin broke into laughter. Nick flushed, and angrily cut into the meat on his plate.

After dinner, seated around the fireplace, Nick brought up the killing of Sleazy.

"That's terrible, simply awful," Kimberly Potts said. "Don't tell me it's starting again."

"What do you mean?" Nick asked.

"We have a real problem in Mill Harbor," Bowen Stirner said through his ever present pipe. "We've had it off and on for several years. It's about time something was done about it."

"A problem?" Nick said.

George Potts spoke up. "Almost every one of us has

had a pet killed around here. Nobody knows what the hell it is that's doing it."

Christine and Nick looked at each other. "I spoke to the police about it," Christine stated. "They think it's some nut."

"He's a strong nut," Nick added. "He twisted that poor mutt's head right off." There was an uneasy silence in the room.

Bowen Stirner's eyes narrowed thoughtfully. "Are you sure of that?"

"Sure as hell," Nick replied. "I saw it. The police pathologist verified it."

Karl Anderson raised a drink in his large hand and spoke to it. "And what great Island Beast, going bump in the night, slouches toward Mill Harbor?"

George Potts stood up. "I saw this scene in a movie once. Now I'm supposed to say, 'It could be any one of us.'" There was nervous laughter.

Bowen Stirner did not smile. "No, it couldn't be one of us. The effort required for manual decapitation would indicate a strength far greater than a human being's."

"Who says it's human?" The voice of Ursala Hauser, seated on the floor near the fireplace, brought another silence to the room.

"Say, lady," Kimberly Potts said finally, "if you're trying to scare me, you're doing a damn good job."

"Ursala, Ursala." Stirner shook his head. "You'll have to excuse her. She's helping me with some research for a book I'm writing on ancient mythologies. I think it's gone to her head."

"I am simply trying to find a logical explanation to your problem. Something was done that could not possibly have been done by a human. However, it was done. Ergo, it must have been done by a nonhuman."

"What sort of nonhuman did you have in mind?" George Potts asked with heavy sarcasm.

The girl ignored his tone. "Your choices are varied. Witches, vampires, goblins, elves, demons, trolls."

"What the hell is a troll?" It was Potts again.

The girl clasped her knees. "In Norse mythology they were a race of huge misshapen creatures who lived in caves of ice and fire. They had the strength of giants because they descended from giants. Grendel, in the Beowulf legend, was a troll. He held Vikings up by their ankles and chewed or twisted their heads off to suck their blood."

"As long as he was Catholic," George Potts interrupted.

"Shut up, George," Stirner admonished. "She's only trying to help."

The girl continued calmly. "There is little evidence of their existence today, however. The Abominable Snowman and the Sasquatch, if they exist, would be trolls."

George Potts jumped up excitedly and pointed a finger at Drogin. "Ergo!" he said. "I've got it. It's him! He's abominable. He killed the dog because it refused his attentions."

Maynard Drogin looked at him steadily. "You're drunk, George."

"I wish I was," Potts said. "She's making me nervous, damnit."

Karl Anderson leaned forward, picking his teeth

with his finger. "It doesn't hold water, little lady," he said. "Assuming this whole conversation is not ridiculous, I detect a fallacy. How can you have descendants of giants, these—what did you call them—trolls, if there are no such things as giants nor ever were?"

The girl and Bowen Stirner exchanged glances. "You are entering an interesting area, Karl," Stirner said. "A major portion of the work we've been doing concerns giantology. The more research we do, the spookier it gets." He paused to relight his pipe. The conversations in the various parts of the room had stopped. Everyone gathered around the small group with Stirner and the girl at its center. "Do you know," he began through the smoke, "that almost every culture in the world has its giants, including our own? We are fascinated by creatures of gigantic strength and proportions. Look at your comics, your movies. The Incredible Hulk, Superman, Godzilla and all his friends, Frankenstein. How many times has each one of you seen *King Kong*? Hollywood knows where we're at. Size and power fascinate all of us."

"I hate to be the one to break this to you, Doc," George Polls said, "but all those muscle types. They're not real, Doctor. They're make-believe."

"Sure they are. The giants are gone. My question to you is—were they ever here? If they weren't, why are there myths about them in every corner of the earth? Did every ancient, separate, uncommunicating culture invent the same fantasy? Or did these myths form around a kernel of reality? Are they more memory than fantasy?"

"I don't buy this every-corner-of-the-globe bit," Potts said. "The only giant I ever heard of lived on the top of a beanstalk, my scientist friend."

Stirner shrugged his shoulders. Suddenly he said, "You *do* believe in the Bible, don't you, George?"

"Yeah. For the most part. So what?"

Stirner's eyes remained steadily on Potts. "Do you have a Bible, Drogin?" he said.

As Maynard Drogin went upstairs for a Bible, Christine felt a tension in the air. They're taking this seriously, she thought. George Potts was chewing his cigar with impatience, his wife looked nervous, almost frightened. Karl Anderson was regarding Bowen Stirner, impassive, thoughtful, his ice blue eyes glittering behind his cigarette. Christine looked at Nick. He was staring unseeing into the empty fireplace. She reached for his hand and held it, but his expression did not change.

Drogin returned and handed a small black book to Bowen Stirner. As he thumbed through, Potts stamped out his cigar in agitation.

Finally Stirner found what he was looking for.

"First Samuel, chapter seventeen, verses four through seven. 'And there went out a man baseborn from the camp of the Philistines named Goliath, of Gath, whose height was six cubits and a span. And he had a helmet of brass upon his head, and he was clothed with a coat of mail with scales, and the weight of his coat of mail was five thousand sicles of brass. And he had greaves of brass on his legs, and a buckler of brass covered his shoulders. And the staff of his spear was like a weaver's beam, and the head of his spear weighed six hundred sicles of iron. And his armour bearers went before him.'

"According to this, Potts, Goliath was approximately ten feet tall, his armor weighed anywhere from two to three hundred pounds, plus his shield, plus his spear 'like a weaver's beam,' the tip of which weighed about twenty-five pounds."

As George Potts squinted at him with belligerent attention, Bowen Stirner flipped through the pages of the book. "The Bible often refers to men of abnormal strength and stature," he continued. "The Anakims, the Rephaim. The gentleman who interests me most, however, is Sampson. Although he did not have gigantic stature, he possessed the strength of a giant. He may be an ancestor to our pet-hating friend out there. Ah, here we are. Listen. Judges, chapter fourteen, verses five and six. 'And when they were come to the vineyards of the town, behold a young lion met him raging and roaring. And the spirit of the Lord came upon Sampson, and he tore the lion as he would have torn a kid in pieces having nothing at all in his hand.'" Stirner looked around the room in the uncomfortable silence that followed. "How interesting your faces are. Blatantly paradoxical. You neither believe me nor want me to continue. I don't blame you on either account."

Maynard Drogin sighed. Finally he spoke. "Remind me, Bowen, to invite you to another one of my parties at some future time, will you? You certainly are a fun person."

"Now how the hell," Kimberly Potts said, "am I supposed to walk home with spaghetti arms here, when there is some misshapen Sampson lurking out there who most probably just loves virgins?"

"'Spaghetti arms'!" George Potts protested, wounded.

"Quiet, honey," Kimberly Potts said, "it could have been worse."

Karl Anderson leaned back against his chair, looking at Bowen Stirner speculatively. "Dr. Stirner," he said, "you are an interesting man. Not accurate, but interesting." His cold blue eyes were heavily lidded.

Walking home under a starlit sky, the moon bright on the trees, Christine linked her arm with Nick's. He seemed distracted, lost in thought. They did not talk. A moonstruck rustling of the rushes made her grasp Nick's arm momentarily. She started to say something but was stopped by the unaccustomed strangeness in his eyes, his face.

As they passed the Anderson boathouse, with its boarded windows and gaping black entrance, Nick disengaged his arm and walked over to its crumbling stone foundation. Christine continued on for several yards before turning around to wait for him. What she saw widened her eyes, drew her hand up to her mouth. Nick was walking toward her, an alien, cunning look on his face. Draped around his neck was a long black snake, its head raised to Nick's eye level, its tongue flicking rapidly in and out.

"Nick!" Christine whispered hoarsely.

As he continued to walk toward her, she saw that his penis was hanging out of the fly of his pants, and that his tongue was going rapidly in and out in unison with the reptile's. Christine turned and ran.

7

The bitter argument that had begun the night before was continued the next morning at breakfast.

"I tell you it was a joke, baby," Nick said. "Since when can't you take a joke?"

"That was some joke, Mister. You scared the hell out of me."

"I must have been drunk. I hardly remember it."

"You weren't drunk, Buster," Christine said evenly. "You were a cold sober practical joker."

"My name is Nick. Buster must be the guy you fuck around with while I'm at work. And I'd rather be a joker than a neurotic, tight-assed bitch." He slammed the door. Christine heard the tires churning stones in the driveway. She began to cry softly. She and Nick had had arguments before, but she had never seen him so cold, so brutal.

A face, covered with skin cream, appeared at the door. "Any coffee left, tight-ass?"

Christine cried harder. "Henrietta, it's not funny," she sobbed.

"Everything's funny. Pour me some coffee and tell me about it."

When Christine had finished relating the incident of the previous night, the older woman adjusted her wig thoughtfully. "That doesn't sound like Nick. Aunt Henrietta will have to snoop into this. I don't watch ten hours of detective shows a week for nothing. Oh, by the way, just to keep my diary accurate, how do you spell 'neurotic'?"

"You're a big help," Christine said, still sniffling.

A fleeting look of tenderness passed over Henrietta's face. She put a hand lightly on Christine's shoulder. "I'm going upstairs and put my face in some semblance of order. We'll talk some more when I'm pretty."

Christine dragged through her work, disspirited, red-eyed. Finally, around noon, she called the restaurant in Cold Spring Harbor. It was Loreto Marino who answered.

"Good afternoon. Villa Marino."

"How come you don't talk nice and sweet like that all the time?" Christine said.

"Christine! *Madonna mia.*"

"How are things at Villa Fiasco?"

"The price of shrimp is killing me. I'm a poor man, Christine."

"I'll bet. Loreto, is Nick there?"

"No, he's out buying lobsters. The price of lobsters is killing me. Say, what's the matter with your husband this last week? He's rude to the customers, he fights with his brothers, he curses, he fires my best waitress. I'm going bankrupt and he's firing my waitresses."

In the background, Christine heard Alfredo's voice. "I told her she should have married me. Then she'd know what fulfillment is," Nick's brother said.

"Sure," Loreto said, "be a bum on the back of a motorcycle. Go put the silverware back, bum. Christine, you want Nick to call you when he comes in?"

"Yes. Good-bye, Pop."

Nick did not call.

At five o'clock, Christine heard his car come into the driveway. I love him, she thought, and I hate fighting. She waited for him to come through the door.

Nick did not come into the house. She watched through the window as he walked along the shore path toward the Andersons', his bathing suit slung over his shoulder. A sudden thought came to her. She went upstairs and put on her new bikini bathing suit. She looked in the mirror approvingly. The first smile of the day crossed her lips. Gathering up a large towel, she hurried downstairs and headed across the lawn toward the Anderson pool.

As she walked past the boathouse and across the uncut lawn toward the rambling house, the sound of a soft, wordless, female voice reached her ears. Christine had never heard anything so beautiful. She assumed it was a radio. But when she rounded the corner of the house, she saw the singer stretched on a redwood lounge. Nick was lying on the stones at her side, his wet head resting on her thigh. The three of them remained motionless for a moment, Christine's mouth partly open, the other two staring at her coldly, like an unfortunate photograph tucked in the back of an album. Finally, Nick sprang up and went to her.

"I'm not intruding, am I, honey?" Christine said, her voice low and strained. "Tell me if I'm intruding."

"Don't be silly, Chris," Nick said, his arm around her shoulder. "This is Karla Anderson, Karl's daughter. She's teaching me how to play the guitar."

Christine looked at the girl closely. She was beautiful. She could not believe that this was Karl Anderson's daughter. The girl was certainly not what Christine had imagined. How could anyone have a body like that, a nose like that? The blue Nordic eyes shone like icebergs with the sun shining through them. They were looking at Christine with a thinly veiled displeasure. She's mad at *me*, Christine thought. Anger swelled within her.

"Are you a good teacher, Miss Anderson?" she said matter-of-factly.

The girl continued to stare at her, smiling with her mouth only. She strummed the guitar once.

"Say, that was really good," Christine said. "Oh, by the way, on what page of the manual is the head-on-the-thigh position?" The blue Anderson eyes glittered at Christine, who stared back unwaveringly. "I'll bet you're a real professional. Aren't you? But Nick, he's my husband here, doesn't have much time for the pros. He's got his hands full with little old amateur me. You know, husband mine, I don't think I'll go swimming after all. That water looks . . . impure. So nice to meet you, Miss Anderson. Coming, hubby?"

Nick looked up at the sky in exasperation and followed Christine across the lawn. Christine caught a final glimpse of the girl as she turned to go. She was sitting rigidly tense, her eyes blue-bright with fury, her mouth turned down like a Greek tragedy mask. It was a face of pure anger. Christine turned away, shaken.

Dinner was a listless affair. Too tired to fight, Nick and Christine had called an unspoken truce. At midnight they took Attila for a walk along the shore. As always, Christine was reassured by the dog's great black shape gliding along beside her in the darkness. The stars shone in summer brightness. There was no wind. Suddenly, the dog stopped in front of them, his ears pressed forward. Then they heard it, too. A low rumble of thunder came to them across the star-strewn water.

Nick looked up. "That's funny," he said. "There isn't a cloud in the sky."

8

*T*he telephone didn't ring until after Nick had left for work. It was Kimberly Potts. Her voice sounded breathless, excited.

"Something's happened across the cove, Chris. The place is crawling with police cars. I can see them from here. I called the station but they wouldn't tell me anything. Have you heard anything?"

"No," Christine said, looking out the kitchen window. "I can see them, too. There must be fifty cops there."

"I mean, it's frightening," Kimberly Potts said.

"After all that nonsense that crazy Bowen was feeding us the other night. I mean, I'm actually lying here in bed, looking at the window, expecting this huge eye to be staring in at me."

"It's a nice neighborhood you have here," Christine said. "I was better off in New York with the muggers and rapists."

"A giant rapist has possibilities. I must discuss it with my therapist this morning. That is, if someone hasn't picked up my car and walked away with it."

"That's not funny, Kim. I'm a little scared."

"So am I. Let me know if you hear any news at all."

Fifteen minutes later, Bowen Stirner drove up in front of the house. Christine led him out to the terrace and brought the coffee with her. His face was pale, distraught.

"Have you heard?" he said.

"Kimberly told me something happened on the other side of the cove."

"Something happened, all right. Two teenagers were murdered."

"Oh my God," Christine gasped.

"There's a little beach over there. The teenagers use it as a lovers' lane. These kids were . . . were attacked right in their car. They . . ." He stopped.

"Tell me, Bowen. I live here. I have a right to know."

"The police won't tell you a thing. But I spoke to Alex Agagian—he lives right next to the beach. He heard it. He's the one who found them. Are you sure you want to hear this?"

"Go on," Christine urged.

"Well, Alex . . . Alex said the car looked like a slaughterhouse. A slaughterhouse, Christine. And he said something I don't understand. One of the doors had been ripped off. And something smashed the windshield and lifted the front half of the roof up. The whole car was torn and twisted . . ."

Christine stared at him. A slow horror started somewhere within her and spread a chill throughout her veins. She shivered. She thought of Joey.

It was Christine who broke the silence. "What are we dealing with here, Bowen?" she asked quietly.

"I wish to hell I knew," he said. He put his hand over hers impulsively. Their eyes met and held. He rose slowly and kissed her cheek. "They'll find him, Chris. They'll find the son of a bitch."

After he had gone, Christine sat there, her mind crowded with emotions. She dialed the police station and was told that Lieutenant Broderick was just walking in the door.

"Mrs. Marino. What can I do for you?" His voice sounded subdued, tired.

"I was just wondering about all the police cars across the cove," Christine said.

"We've had a double homicide, Mrs. Marino." She heard a voice calling his name in the background. "I have to go," he said. "We'll keep all you folks out there informed as soon as we know anything."

"Do you have any leads, any suspects?" Christine's voice was low.

"Yes, we think we know who it is." The man sounded exhausted.

Christine's heart leaped. "Can you tell me who you think . . . I mean, anything at all?"

"I can't be sure, Mrs. Marino. We do have an APB out. Our evidence indicates that someone has been living in the woods around here for at least a month. He's been seen several times and his description checks."

"Checks? Checks with what?"

"The suspect is criminally insane, Mrs. Marino. He escaped from Pilgrim State Hospital on June second. I understand he's a bad one. Man named Charles Steinmetz."

"What should we do? I mean is it safe to go out of the house?"

"We are telling everyone to continue all normal activities. Our men are posted over this entire area. If he's still around, we'll apprehend him. Meanwhile, it wouldn't hurt to keep that dog with you. Excellent deterrent. What? Yeah. I have to go, Mrs. Marino. Don't worry. We'll get him." He hung up.

Christine felt strangely relieved. At least here was something concrete. She knew who was out there, even if it was a maniac. So much for Bowen Stirner and giants and goblins and trolls. Terrific, she thought. I'm relieved that it's only a criminally insane maniac out there. Terrific.

At that moment Henrietta swept into the kitchen, complete with makeup, false eyelashes, a huge blond wig with uncountable curls, and her glasses held casually in one hand. She looked around, disappointed. "Where is that beautiful man?" she said.

Christine looked at her aunt for a long moment, at the earrings with a pair of dice hanging from each ear, at the incredible eyelashes, at the wig which was never on straight. The tensions of the past few days plus her fear of the man in the woods welled up in her all at once and she broke into uncontrolled, hysterical laughter. Henrietta, looking like a disgruntled, senile doll, watched her with mock distaste. Christine tried to stop but could not.

"If you don't stop it this instant, I'm packing," Henrietta said, pushing the wig haughtily over to the other side of her head. This action sent Christine shrieking out of the kitchen to collapse on the living room couch. Henrietta followed her, trying not to laugh herself. "Stop it, you rude little girl. Show some respect."

Christine finally brought herself under control and stood up to embrace her aunt. "Oh, Hen," she said. "I'm not laughing at you. I love you. It's just, I don't know, it's just everything. I'm having trouble with Nick, which you know all about by listening at doors . . ."

"Every word is in my diary."

"And now this detective tells me there's a killer maniac running around the woods out there." She told Henrietta what she had learned that morning, leaving out the more lurid details.

The older woman's eyes narrowed. "Nice neighborhood you've got here. Where's the dog? I'm staying by the dog." They smiled at each other, a little uncertainly.

It was after three o'clock when Christine had her second caller of the day. Standing in the doorway, wiping his thick neck with a handkerchief, was Karl Anderson.

Christine's body tensed. She stared at him coldly. "Yes? What is it?"

"I shall nobly dispense with our usual salutation," he said, "and get right to the point. It's hot, it's humid. I want a new, more meaningful relationship between us. In a word, I am inviting you to swim in our pool. We could share a drink together, get off on a new foot, as they say."

Christine stood there, speechless. This was not a day she would want to repeat. "Thank you, Mr. Anderson, but I simply must get my baking done."

"Why don't you call me Karl?"

"I don't want to," Christine replied flatly.

"Then 'Mr. Anderson' it shall be. Say, I have a wonderful idea. We could have that drink right here. Actually, I don't swim very much."

"Actually, I don't bake at all," Christine said. This was too ridiculous, she thought. This repulsive Viking is making a pass at me. "But while we're on the subject of swimming," she continued, "I would appreciate it if the poolside guitar lessons were discontinued."

"Ah. That would be Karla. Has she been flirting with your handsome husband? Insatiable woman. I'm afraid it's a family trait of ours, insatiability." Those eyes of ice pierced her momentarily, then looked away. "Your husband is a grown man, Mrs. Marino. Christine. I cannot stop him from coming over, if that is his . . . desire. But you have my solemn word. Whenever he is there, I shall be in attendance. I promise you." He was looking at her breasts as he spoke. Christine looked over his shoulder for Attila. Where is that dog, she thought.

"You've heard about the recent unpleasantness?" he continued.

"Yes."

"It will pass," he said, shrugging his bulky shoulders.

Joey Marino came hurtling down the stairs. Anderson's eyes left Christine reluctantly. He looked down at Joey as if he had just bitten into a lemon and was trying not to show it.

Ye gods, Christine thought. On top of everything else, he doesn't like children. Ye gods. Instinctively, she held Joey's shoulders close to her. The gesture was not lost on Anderson.

"You don't like neighbor Karl very much, do you, Mrs. Marino?"

"I'm afraid not, neighbor."

"But why not?" He sounded almost petulant. There was something deep in his eyes that Christine could not fathom.

Christine made a small, helpless gesture. "I . . . you . . . you're not nice, that's all."

"'Nice'?" The glacial eyes looked truly puzzled. "But

I *am* nice. My hair is parted, I wear expensive cologne. I pay my taxes quarterly. I even have a mother. Of course I'm nice."

"No, you're not," Christine said soberly. "You make me feel like a rabbit in the middle of an open field, while you sit there like a hungry, salivating coyote."

"No briar patch to run to?"

"Precisely."

"But my dear Mrs. Marino. That type of thinking is ridiculous."

"You think so, do you?"

"But of course." The wild smile again. "Because, dear lady, there is not a briar patch in the world that could keep me out." He looked at his watch. "Well, it would be nice to chat all day, but I really must be going. A jeweler's life is not his own. We must do this again sometime." He waved two fingers at them and strode out of the house.

Christine stared after the huge man. Joey, looking up into his mother's face, was frightened by the look he saw there.

Later that afternoon Christine, Henrietta, and Joey walked down to the shore, Attila trailing after them. As Henrietta and Joey went wading, Christine stretched herself out to the sun on a folding chair. She found it difficult to relax. The events of the last few weeks raced through her mind like storm clouds gathering over a desert. Nick, her love, her safe harbor, her old reliable, had changed. There was no question about it. There had been disagreements and fights before this. But always they had ended quickly, and she and Nick had been more deeply in love than before. This time it was different. They had not spoken much since the incident at the pool over a week ago. Nick had grown sullen, cold. He seemed preoccupied. Their sex life had lost its joy. She would not deny him, but he seemed callous now, demanding. There was no tenderness. His sense of humor, the delight of Christine's life, had all but disappeared. Christine was perplexed and troubled. Was it that bikinied bitch? Was it Christine herself? She could understand nothing, explain nothing.

And then there was her new neighbor, a madman named Steinmetz, who roamed the woods where Joey played. Christine allowed a thought to surface that she had kept suppressed since the death of Sleazy. Run, flee, get the hell out of here. Sell the house. Avoid pain. Avoid terror. Life should be cozy, comfortable, safe. Life should not include a maniac in the bulrushes. She stroked Attila's head as he lay alongside of her, his tongue lolling in the heat.

As the sun beat down on her oil-slicked body, Christine decided that she was a coward. That she had been a coward for as long as she could remember. She had been one in sixth grade when Priscilla Dowdy, a head shorter than she was and skinny, had challenged her to a fight and Christine had walked away. She had been a coward at fourteen when she had fallen off that horse and had refused to get back on. She could still remember the look on her father's face. That Connecticut squire would have personally found, manacled, and prosecuted to the fullest extent of the law friend Steinmetz long ago. Christine's appearance, she knew, had been her shell, her protection. Since her teens men had done things for her, taken care of her. Why confront life when a man would do it for you? She remembered her father's words on the eve of their wedding. "Nick, ever since Christine was a little girl, it has been my greatest joy to care for her, protect her. I wish I could turn the clock back twenty years and do it all over again, but I can't. Now it's your turn, Nick. I'm counting on you."

A lump came into Christine's throat as she thought of her father, who had died a year after their wedding. Nick had certainly taken her father's message to heart. Her strong, fiery husband had taken care of her for the past ten years, shielded her well. She needed him and lying there in the sun she began to realize just how much.

Of course, lady, she told herself, there is another option. You could always grow up. You could try taking care of yourself, take a stand, stop thinking about running away. It's called coping with life. The sun glowed crimson through Christine's eyelids, the salt air washed over her body. I will try it, she told herself firmly. Pretty soon now.

At her side the dog suddenly raised his head. He was looking at the rushes and tangled undergrowth several yards behind where Christine lay. A deep growl began in his throat. Christine's eyes opened and stared into the bright sky. Alarm that quickly turned to fear tensed her body. She turned her head. The feathery tops of the rushes were swaying slightly. Had someone disturbed them or was it the wind? She couldn't tell. The dog was standing now and barking fiercely. Christine put his leash on. She had difficulty holding him. Henrietta and Joey came splashing back to see what the trouble was.

"I think we'll go back now," Christine said, keeping her voice calm.

"Aw, Mom." Joey made a face.

"Come on, honey. I've got to start dinner now."

Henrietta looked at her closely. She turned to Joey. "Come on, dearie," she said. She took his hand firmly and started toward the house. The dog continued to bark furiously and was lunging toward the rushes. Only Christine's sharp, repeated commands and tight hold on the leash stopped him from an attack.

After they had reached home, the dog was still agitated. Christine brought him inside, hugged him, and set out his dinner. Henrietta walked into the kitchen and watched her thoughtfully.

"What was that all about, Christine?" she asked.

"Most probably nothing. Attila started barking. I got panicky, I suppose. It most probably was one of Lieutenant Broderick's men. They're posted all over, he said. It could even have been a rabbit."

Henrietta looked at the dog, which still had not quieted down. "Some rabbit," she said. She pushed her wig forward. "I think I'll have a drink. Join me?"

"Absolutely," Christine said.

Christine and Nick sat silently on the terrace after dinner watching the rose-colored sea gulls soar in the setting sun. She glanced at him now and then as he stared dreamily over the water. We're getting old, she thought. Or fat. The hard lines of Nick's face had softened perceptibly, his body had lost some of its leanness. God, how she loved him.

"I love you, fatso," she said.

Nick swiveled his head and looked at her. His eyes blinked several times. "What?" he said sharply.

"I said, do you think it will rain, even if it *is* Tuesday?"

"What the hell are you talking about, Chris?" He looked at her with impatience.

Christine was determined not to argue. "Nick," she said, "what's wrong with us? We're not as splendid together as we used to be. What is it, Nick?"

He stared at her. Bewilderment and a flash of pain were etched on his face for a brief moment. "I wish I knew, Chris," he said. He looked out over the water again.

Christine spoke as calmly as she could. "Is it that girl, Nick? Are you in love with her?"

Nick did not look at her. He seemed to be struggling with his words. "I love *you*, Christine. I love Joey. I love you both . . . so much."

Quick tears came to Christine's eyes. She reached over and touched his hand. As she did so, a shudder seemed to pass through him. A dark shadow settled on his face. He turned his head and looked at her, his eyes sincere, burning.

"Do you know what I love about you most, my beloved?" he said.

"Tell me, Nick."

"Your cunt," he said. The words came out flat, hard. "Give me your cunt, Christine."

Christine stared at him, her mouth open. Then shock, anger, and a deep hurt made her slap him across the face as hard as she could. She ran into the house, up the stairs, and slammed the door to their bedroom.

9

From the diary of Henrietta Knapp:

July 12.

Splitting headache. Must remember never to mix vodka and Chianti before dinner. After dinner iffy, too.

I must have missed a beauty last night. Not speaking to each other at breakfast. Christine's eyes as red as mine.

Took Joey to look for steamer clams in A.M. Christine insisted we take that brute dog along. Am getting too attached to that kid.

What a life!!!

July 13.

They are still at it. At least she has stopped crying. Tried to talk to Nick and got insulted for my troubles. Shall not get involved!!!

Dr. Stirner stopped by again. Nobody should be that handsome. Still asking Christine to go sailing. She didn't go.

That lunatic has still not been caught. Although police everywhere, we still do not go out without that dog. Plus, I have a long hatpin in my wig. Lunatic beware!!!

July 14.

Love blooms in strange gardens. That large, steely-eyed squid, Anderson, sent Christine two dozen roses today. The card had a picture of a rabbit on it. She threw them in the garbage. Lots of playboys around here. Un neighborhood incroyable.

July 15.

Bad news!!! Am getting allergic to scotch. Half a bottle and my whole body seems to fall apart. Incredible symptoms!

The war goes on. The master of the house went swimming in Anderson's pool after work today. The mistress slammed around the kitchen like a caged leopard, burned the roast, and said words I cannot repeat in this diary.

Something not kosher here. A little police work by yours truly is in order.

July 16.

Had to feed the swimmer myself last night. Came

in around ten, strange look in his eyes. I love that man almost as much as I love Chris and Joey, but he's changed. Eats like someone raised with wolves, hair too long, face bloated. He's not old smoothie Nick anymore. Really worried about him.

July 17.
Definitely going on the wagon! Just stubbed my toe dancing in my room. The pain is not to be believed!!!
Three of us finally going sailing with beautiful Dr. Stirner tomorrow. Joey talked her into it and Chris said she had something she wanted to ask him.
Wig, parasol, sheer dress already laid out. Set alarm for four o'clock to start makeup. Let the chips fall where they may!!!!
Good night, Frank Sinatra, wherever you are!

10

The sails billowed above Christine in the morning sunlight. The air was fresh and clear, almost cold. As the boat hissed quietly through the inlet that led to Long Island Sound, she looked at the shorelines on either side of her. Steep sand cliffs led up from the rock-strewn shore toward rolling lawns that spilled out from the houses above them. Sun-browned children clambered over a stone jetty in the distance, squealing with delight. Christine watched them for a moment and turned her eyes to Joey, who was clutching the rope that controlled the jib, his eyes eager with excitement.

To hell with trouble, she thought, putting her head back to catch the sun. The madman shall be caught and returned to the woodwork. And Nick, my once and future darling . . . Her thoughts were interrupted by screams of laughter. Bowen Stirner's name was called out several times. She opened her eyes to see three young girls racing along beside them in a small catamaran. She looked at Stirner through narrowed eyes and nodded her head knowingly. He shrugged his shoulders. "Fans," he explained.

Christine continued to look at him as he glanced up into the sails. He looked like something you wanted to take home, this Dr. Stirner. Bronzed, white shirt open to the waist, even his pipe was pretty.

Stirner caught her speculative look. "I make quite a picture when the sun hits me just right, don't I?" he said. "It's all calculated. Female adulation, in my case, is inevitable."

"I was just comparing you with my husband," Christine said. "You came in third."

"Third?"

"Yes. Nick, Karl Anderson, and then yourself."

Stirner winced. "Women on board are bad luck, right matey?" he said to Joey.

"Right" was the quick reply.

Henrietta had opened the cooler on the seat next to her and was peering in. "Let's watch the banter," she said. "Everything that gets said or done gets reported directly to Nick and recorded in my diary. Is that white wine I see?"

"Yes," Stirner said. "Shall we open it now?"

"By all means." Henrietta plunged her hand into the ice and brought out a shimmering bottle.

Bowen Stirner leaned across Christine's legs. "I'm sure there's an opener in there somewhere."

"No problem at all," Henrietta said. She fished in her bag and immediately came up with a corkscrew.

As he drew back, Stirner's hand rested on Christine's knee for an instant.

"Careful!" she said loudly. "I'm sure our chaperone is watching us."

"Like a hawk," Henrietta said, inspecting the label on the bottle. "If this isn't a month old, I'm not drinking it. Ah, a very interesting number."

"What's that?" Christine asked.

"Twelve percent alcohol."

While Christine and Bowen Stirner sipped at their wine, Henrietta finished several glasses hurriedly. When only a small amount was left in the bottle, she put it to her mouth and drained it.

Christine watched her. "Want a paper bag, auntie dear?"

"Have some respect for your betters," Henrietta said. She burped delicately and held the bottle up. "That's a very interesting little wine," she said.

Bowen Stirner looked at her in amazement. "There's another bottle in there somewhere, dear lady. Please help yourself."

Christine smiled and trailed her hand in the rushing water. "You know, Bowen, you really had me a little frightened the other night. All that talk about giants. That's what I wanted to talk to you about. You didn't really believe a word you were saying, did you?"

"I did and I do. Not the giants in the fairy tales, whose heads were in the clouds. Too big. Improbable. But I am firmly convinced that some time in prehistory a race of beings did exist who attained a height of ten, twenty, even thirty feet."

Henrietta looked at them, one eye almost closed. "Giants?" she said. "Poppycock. Pure, unadulterated poppycock." She stared into her glass. "I am on a ship of fools."

"On the contrary, my dear woman," Stirner said. "It is an anthropological probability. We choose not to believe because it frightens and disturbs us to do so."

"But, dearie, where are they?"

"Gone, Mrs. Knapp. Gone with the brontosaurus, the woolly mammoth, the dodo bird. Natural selection is a harsh master. They were not fit. In the case of giant hominoids, I think an additional force was at work."

"What was that?" Christine asked.

"Intermarriage."

Henrietta's eyes flew open. "Intermarriage! You mean that all the giants were Jewish?"

"I am referring to . . ."

"Hispanic?"

"I am referring to intermarriage with *Homo habilis*. Man. Us, dear lady."

"Protestants?"

"Henrietta!" Christine looked at her in exasperation. She turned toward Stirner. "Why would they want to, well, mate with us, Bowen?"

"The gods and giants are attracted to us, my dear."

"What gods? What giants? Where?" Henrietta said.

"Many gods. Everywhere. The Greek gods mated mortal women with the consistency of minks. Demigods, heroes with superhuman strength, were the result. Hercules, Perseus, Achilles. Men, with the strength of giants. The Hindu gods knew mortal women. The gods of Norse mythology lusted after human women and men on a regular basis. Their progeny were many. Milton, in his *Paradise Regained* has Satan say to Belial:

> *Before the flood, then with thy lusty crew*
> *False-titled sons of God, roaming the earth,*
> *Cast wanton eyes on the daughters of men*
> *And coupled with them and begot a race.*

"Even that old devil himself, Satan, has been attracted to the female hominoid in countless legends and stories. And why not?" He relit his pipe and looked directly at Christine. "Consider the sublime divinity of the human face," he said. "If I were a god, or a devil, or a giant, I would be tempted, sorely tempted."

"Hold it right there, dearie." Henrietta's empty glass came down hard on top of the cooler. "Not on my ship you don't."

Stirner shook his head patiently and continued. "Speaking in the vernacular of the ancients, for obvious reasons, it takes two to tango . . ."

"I used to tango," Henrietta said.

"Precisely. We hominoids are not guiltless, you know. We are a highly sexed species. The male sexual organ is by far the largest, in ratio to body size, of all the primates. Our female knows no estrus, being ready and willing on a perpetual basis . . ."

"Wrong, Professor," Henrietta said. "Without music, a good Chianti . . ."

"A perpetual basis, I repeat. Knowing this, and taking what must be an accurate guess at the inestimable power of the sex drive of those whom we call giants, it was inevitable that the two related species would couple on a furious basis. The result is that there is a strong possibility that the descendants of these prehistoric unions walk the earth today. We humans have given them their comparatively minute size, their increased brain power. The giants have given them their incalculable strength, their magic, their . . . temperament."

"I don't believe you for a moment," Christine said. "I cannot. If what you say were to be true, it would be terrifying."

"The world is a terrifying place, Christine," Stirner said, his voice low, musing. "It runs red. The tiger rends, the shark mutilates. It operates without pity. Is the constrictor ever conscience stricken? Does the crocodile regret? It is only the constructs of human society that shelter us from the mad, implacable violence of Nature, that weave a web of make-believe over our eyes. When some elemental force tears this web, we shudder. But it was there all the time. Do you think what happened to your dog or those two kids would raise an eyebrow in the jungle? The being I suggest is no more terrifying than a praying mantis, a weasel. Accept the reality of what they do and my creature is simply one terror among many."

Christine shivered in the bright sunlight. "Why do you keep talking about this beast of yours? Don't you ever discuss baseball statistics or crabgrass?"

"On occasion. But events have a way of adding up. And there is something going on in Mill Harbor that adds up wrong."

"It all adds up," Christine said firmly, "to an ordinary, everyday lunatic. His name is Steinmetz, and he hates animals."

"And teenagers?" Christine had never seen him look so serious. "Can he rip cars apart? Tear a dog's head from its body? Something is wrong. Something doesn't categorize." He puffed his pipe in silence.

Christine sighed. "Dr. Stirner, mine host. You are ruining a lovely day. You seem to dote on terror. Speak to me of sailing, of your years before the mast."

Stirner smiled. "Replace the web, dear sir," he said. "Is that it?"

"You want to know what terror is, dearie?" It was Henrietta, who had been listening hazily. "We're out of wine."

Christine laughed and gave her body to the baking rays of the sun. But she could not relax. There was an unease within her that had not been there before.

As Christine sat brushing her hair that night, she saw Nick looking at her in the dressing table mirror. He was lying on top of the covers, smoking a cigarette. She recognized that look. Despite her anger, despite everything, it still excited her.

"How was the sailing?" he asked.

"Fine. Joey loved it."

"Is he a good sailor, the professor?"

"Yes." A long pause.

"Do visions of sugarplums dance in your head?"

"What do you mean, Nick?"

"The eminent sugarplum. Does he dance in your head?"

Christine met his eyes in the mirror. "I love *you*, Nick. You're my boy."

"Prove it," he said.

Christine's hand stopped. Their eyes locked in the mirror.

"It's been a long time, Chris." His voice was softer now.

The brushing continued methodically. "Yes," she said.

"I need you, Chris. Now. Tonight."

Christine looked down at nothing on her dresser. "Why don't you just go over and take a guitar lesson?"

"No, Chris," Nick said seriously. "You're wrong. I haven't been unfaithful. I . . . I . . . we talk, we do things. Karl is always there. It's not what you think. I want *you*, Chris, I love *you*."

Christine could not raise her eyes. "It's just not that easy, my love. Are you going to tell me again what you love best about me, Nick?"

"I don't know why I said that. I must have been drunk or crazy."

She managed to turn and face him. "No, Nick," she said. "Not drunk. Not crazy. You're my husband and I love you. I can't help that. But something's happened to you, Nick. To us. What is it, Nick? What's wrong?" Her eyes searched his face. It was masked, unreadable.

"There is nothing wrong with me that would not be immediately corrected by holding my wife in my arms where she belongs. You are my joy and my therapy."

Christine looked at him searchingly for a long time. She knew she was going to go to him, but she wanted some reassurance, some evidence of love. Nick was looking down at his cigarette. "All right, Nick," she said, almost sadly. "Give me a minute." His face did not change.

Christine closed the bathroom door behind her and began to undress without enthusiasm. Dressed only in bikini panties, she applied perfume to herself mechanically. She looked at her face in the mirror. You look worried, seductress. That's your husband out there. Smile. It could be Karl Anderson. Perhaps a touch of pale lipstick for the therapist. She leaned forward and applied the brush to her lips carefully.

Behind her, the door opened slowly. In the bathroom mirror Christine saw Nick standing behind her. He had tied her mother's old fox fur around his head, the snout of the animal resting on his forehead. "Mon amour," he said, and advanced toward her.

Christine tried to smile. "Mon idiot," she answered. Nick came up behind her, pulled her panties down to her ankles and grasped both of her arms in his hands. She felt his aroused sexual organ probing, plunging. She tried to find his eyes in the mirror and was met with the black, glassy eyes of the fox. "No, wait, honey. Don't." She raised her voice. "Stop it!" she cried.

Nick's hand drew her right arm around behind her; his left forearm forced her head down into the sink. She could not move. Her pained cries and entreaties were drowned in the bestial grunts that reverberated around the tiled bathroom.

When he had finished, he released her. Christine stood there, her panties around her ankles, her body trembling. She stared at him dully in the mirror. "Get out, you bastard," she whispered. Nick left, slamming the door. Christine did not move. "Oh, you bastard," she said aloud.

When she began to feel again, pain and revulsion filled her. She vomited quietly into the sink. When she had finished, she still could not move from where she stood. "Oh, you bastard," she repeated into the mirror. Her face crumbled before her as sobs convulsed her body.

11

Four days passed in anger and silence. Nick tried several times to apologize, but gave up in the face of Christine's mute fury. He slept in the study. Henrietta did what she could with Joey, but the tension was heavy, palpable. Christine spent her days going stolidly through her housework. She did not paint. She barely talked. She stared out of windows.

On the fifth morning, Loreto Marino called. "Chris, it's Loreto." It was good to hear his solid, familiar voice. "Eh, where's Nick? He's sick?"

"No, Lorry," she said. "He left the house early this morning. Isn't he there?"

"Never showed up. I'm going to dock him for the day. Hey, Chris, what's the matter? You don't sound so good."

Christine welcomed the shoulder. "Oh, Lorry, it's Nick." She tried not to cry. "Something's wrong. I don't know him anymore."

"Whatever it is, Chris, we'll fix it. You and I. My Nicky's a good boy. I wanted to talk to you about him, anyway. You come over here right now. I'll make you something special. We'll talk."

"Lorry, I'm not hungry, I . . ."

"Everybody's hungry. You come down here, *amica*. Right now." He hung up.

Christine nodded at the phone and replaced the receiver. That's a bright thing to do, she thought. Now start talking to the refrigerator. She didn't know whether to laugh or cry. She did both.

The taxi dropped her off in front of the restaurant. She had always loved the Villa Marino in Manhattan with its lush red and gold interior and its abundance of statues. She liked this one even better, however, because she had helped design it. "They tell me out here good food is not enough," Loreto had said. "You need ambience. Lobsters I understand, ambience you understand." Together they had designed a light, airy waterfront setting, complete with hanging gardens and an indoor waterfall. Loreto had insisted on the statues. The main dining room looked out over the water. There were boat slips in front of the parking lot.

Loreto greeted her as soon as she came in. He wore a tuxedo and a fresh carnation day and night. He was a sturdy man, broad shouldered, short, with large powerful hands. His gray hair was thinning at the temples.

"Hello, handsome," Christine said.

Loreto Marino never shook her hand. He embraced her, he kissed her. "*Madonna* Christina. Look at that beautiful face. Alfredo is right. You're too good-looking for Nick." He led her to a small table in the corner. Peering down at them was a large bust with a brass nameplate below it.

"Is that how Nero looked?" Christine said, glancing up at the ugly face.

"What Nero. It's my cousin Georgio. They were both crazy. His daughter, the communist, made it. I had to put it somewhere. Tell me, Chris, what's wrong between you and Nick?"

Christine told him what had occurred during the last few weeks. When she had finished, Loreto looked at her for a long moment. "You didn't tell me everything, right?"

"Well, Lorry, I . . ."

"It's okay. I respect you for it. From what you tell me, this don't sound like my Nick. Nick never did crazy stuff like that before. I don't like this. If I ever saw a marriage made in heaven, it was you two." He pointed at her. "Now I'll tell you something. I think he's having, what do you call it, a breakdown or something. He's been acting funny in the restaurant. Strange. I wasn't going to tell you, but it's getting serious."

"What do you mean 'funny'?"

"Funny is funny. Weird. He does bad things, not nice. You'll forgive me for saying it, he gooses people when he takes them to their table. It sounds funny, it's not. It's okay for an occasional divorcee, give her a break, but men? He did it to children, too. I don't like that."

"Oh, no," Christine said.

"He's either dreaming or fighting. He hit a busboy the other day, a kid, he's going to sue. He fights with the customers. Two waitresses quit because of what he did to them—they wouldn't tell me. That's not my Nick, Chris. You know him. And today he didn't show up at all. He never did anything like that. I had Alfredo taking reservations, that's how bad it was today. Something's happened to my boy, Christine. A breakdown. I'm sure of it. He needs our help."

They talked for fifteen minutes. At the end, Loreto said, "Okay. Between you and me we'll handle it. If he's got to go see a shrink, he goes. You and me, we take care of him."

Christine felt someone's lips at the back of her neck. She turned and looked up at Alfredo. He was as handsome as Nick, but taller, more slender.

"When are you going to leave your husband for me? Why do you fight your feelings like this?" he said. Christine managed to smile.

Loreto Marino tapped his forehead with his hand. "Ah, the mathematician speaks. Today he tried to seat a party of seven at a table for four. I told him to count the chairs. Now he can handle anything up to a party of eight. Go, Beast. Wipe the saliva from that thing you call a moustache and get her some of the manicotti."

"No," Christine protested.

"Yes," he insisted.

She ate the delicious food without enthusiasm, kissed Loreto good-bye, and left the restaurant.

When Christine arrived home, Nick was not in the house. A thought crept into her mind which she fought unsuccessfully. Guitar lessons. She busied herself with Joey and the dinner. Seeing Loreto and Alfredo had made Christine feel better. She remembered how comforting Nick's family had been when they had lived in the city, the wonderful times they had had at the restaurant with Nick's friends. Nick's friends. A sudden thought entered Christine's mind. Maybe they could help him, talk some sense into him. They had always depended on each other in the past, their loyalties unquestioned. Well, he needs them now, she thought.

Christine almost ran to the phone. It was good to hear Sal Valenti's gruff voice again. He enthusiastically agreed to get the boys together and pay Nick a surprise visit the following week. "Peace and quiet revolt me," he said, "but it will be good to see the boy again."

When Christine hung up, she felt better. Until she remembered Nick's absence. I'm going over there, she decided. I don't know what I'll do, but I'm going over there.

She walked through the corral and took the path to the Andersons' house. Halfway there she stopped. A low howling came to her from the trees. Fear jolted through her. She took a few more tentative steps and stopped again. The sound, uncanny, disturbing, seemed to be coming from the boathouse. Christine knew she could go no farther. Cursing her cowardice, she retraced her steps hurriedly, the sound diminishing as she started to run.

She heard Nick come in a little after midnight. Putting on her robe, she went downstairs. I can't go on like this, she thought. End it, change it, I don't want to go on like this.

Nick was bending over as he peered into the refrigerator.

"Nick," she said. "We have to talk. Now. Where have you been? You promised to take Joey to a softball game. I'd like to know where you've been, Nick."

Nick straightened up slowly and turned around. She did not like what she saw. There was something wrong with his eyes. "Aha," he said. "I'll bet you'll want to know where I've been."

"It's after midnight, Nick. Where were you?"

"A good question. An excellent question. A question not easily answered. Your Nick has been to Gillie Furth. I have dined with Vincent, mad Vincent, in an ice palace on the rim of the world. When the sun struck it, we were, both of us, blinded by a beauty that can kill. Then he took my hand and showed me the world before the world. A place of frost and rime and high tarns from which blue cataracts flow. I've suckled on icicles sweeter than your breasts. They run in my veins. Oh, he's definitely mad, that Van Gogh. But we understand each other. We shall meet again. Now tell me, Christine. Is there any chicken left?" He turned again to the refrigerator.

Christine stared at his back. He doesn't look crazy, she thought. He only talks that way. She wondered if he had been drinking.

"Nick, I went to see Loreto today . . ."

"Ah, old Pops. Was he mad? I'll square it with him tomorrow. Let's face it. I took a day off." His voice rose.

"It's not that," Christine said. "We talked about you, Nick. We both think . . . well . . . that you've been acting a little funny."

"You mean . . . I'm not myself?" He smiled.

"Just different, Nick. We thought maybe you'd like to talk to somebody. A professional."

He looked at her carefully. "You think Nick is nuts, is that it?"

"No. We just think you may be . . . having some difficulty. Maybe some sort of . . . breakdown."

After a moment, he said. "You might say that. Yes."

"Will you go see someone, Nick?"

He was taking food out of the refrigerator and putting it on the large, wooden kitchen table. "Sure I'll go," he said.

Christine's heart leaped. "Do you mean it, Nick?"

"Sure I do. Say, I haven't been treating you too well recently, have I, old sport?"

Christine ignored this. "When will you go, Nick?"

He thought for a moment. "At the end of the summer," he said.

"Will you, Nick?"

"Wife, by the end of the summer you won't recognize me. That's a promise." He had completed making a large sandwich and was eyeing it speculatively.

"All right, that's fine," Christine said. "Nick, I . . ."

He looked up at her. There was something in his eyes, something. "Good night, Christine," he said.

The first police sirens began to wail around two o'clock. Christine awoke with a start. Red flashing lights were weaving leaf patterns on the bedroom ceiling. She ran downstairs. Nick was already up, looking out the window next to the front door. Two police cars were in their driveway.

Nick and Christine walked out to the cars. A policeman was standing in front of one of them, a rifle in his hands.

"What is it, officer?" Nick asked. "What's happened?"

The policeman turned to them. His voice was polite but firm. "I'll have to ask you to get back in your house, Mr. Marino. Right now."

"Okay, officer," Nick said. "Just tell us what's going on."

"It's Steinmetz," the officer said. "They've got him surrounded in the Anderson boathouse. Now please get inside."

They stood behind the sliding glass doors of the terrace. Christine's heart was racing. "Nick," she said. "I hope they get him. They've got to get him."

"They will," Nick said. "Too many serpents in Paradise already."

Christine did not even look at him. She had given up trying to fathom him weeks ago. They stood, unspeaking, for several more minutes, when, suddenly, a wordless shrieking shattered the night air. Christine had never heard anything so mad, so terrifying. A thought struck her. My God, that must have been him howling in the boathouse this afternoon. I almost walked right past him. She closed her eyes and took several deep breaths. There was silence among the trees now.

The police radio crackled. Christine recognized the voice of Lieutenant Broderick. "All units. Prisoner in custody. Wrap it up."

Wild elation raced through Christine. A weight of anxiety and fear that she hadn't realized she was carrying lifted from her shoulders. With Nick, she half walked, half ran down the driveway toward the road. There they turned and ran toward the Andersons' house to their right. When they reached their neighbor's driveway they saw five police cars parked in front of it, their lights flashing. Seated in the back of one of them was Steinmetz. Christine got a glimpse of a small, shirtless man. His hands were manacled behind him, his body tensed. Perspiration gleamed on his face. His shaved head was nodding up and down rhythmically. His eyes were fierce and cunning. They swept past Christine and never stopped. The police car started and he was gone.

Christine saw Lieutenant Broderick sitting in another car. She walked over to him, Nick still at her side. "Congratulations, Lieutenant," she said. "You'll never know how happy you've made me, made all of us."

"Did he give you much trouble?" Nick asked.

"Piece of cake," the detective answered. "No gun, no weapon of any kind. Like netting a butterfly." The green eyes were looking with friendly interest down the front of Christine's bathrobe. She pulled her collar closed but did not move. "Nassau's finest," he said reflectively. "Nassau's finest always get their man," he added.

"He didn't look particularly strong to me," Christine pointed out.

The detective looked at her sharply. "Why do you say that, Mrs. Marino?"

"No reason," she said quickly. "I just thought he'd be, I don't know, larger, stronger. I mean after what happened to those teenagers . . ."

"He was strong all right. It took three of us to pry him away from a beam in that boathouse. That's what all that screaming was about. He just didn't want to leave. We've got to go. You folks can rest easy now." He waved his hand as the car sped away. Christine waved back. It's over, she thought. Thank God, it's over.

12

The next week was a time of quiet happiness for Christine. The maniac was gone from her world and, best of all, Nick seemed to change for the better. He did not go to the Andersons'. He played with Joey; he seemed less cold, less hostile. There was still something secretive about his eyes, some undefined change in his attitude, but Christine was thankful for any improvement. His friends were coming in a day or two. She felt sure that this would help him. And he *had* promised to get professional help at the end of the summer.

Kimberly Potts called early one morning while Christine was having coffee with Henrietta. "A party," she said. "A large, seagoing party tomorrow. Everybody in your house *must* come."

"What's the occasion?" Christine asked.

"I'm calling it the Charles Steinmetz Going Away Party and Clambake."

"The what?" Christine began to laugh.

"You heard me. We're going to tie all our boats together, steam clams, and drink as much as possible."

"We don't have a boat," Christine said.

"You're coming with us. Our boat is the biggest. I wouldn't have it any other way. Now, here's what I want you to bring."

After Christine had hung up, Henrietta said, "I'm not going. I simply cannot go. My wig. The blond one with the curls. It's at the hairdressers." Christine walked over and hugged her. Things had returned to normal. "I could go red, of course," Henrietta continued. "Nobody's seen the red one. You can introduce me as your younger sister."

The boat glided powerfully through the sunlit water. Seated on the upper steering deck, Christine watched as Joey helped George Potts steer through the channel markers. Her son's eager, attentive face filled her with pleasure as Potts seriously explained the rules of small craft navigation to him.

"George," she said, "you look almost handsome in that hat. What rank is it—captain?"

"Admiral," he said. "Do you know how much this boat costs? And please don't talk to us while we are on the bridge. If you find yourself uncontrollably attracted by my rank or my teak, we'll discuss it at anchor, not before." He took his hat off and placed it on Christine's head. Joey giggled, but his eyes did not leave the water in front of him.

Down below her Christine could hear Kimberly Potts and Henrietta laugh at something Nick had said. Okay, she thought. This is the way my life is going to be. No more crazies. No more fear. And my Nick. My sane, funny, beloved Nick. The way he used to be. She raised her chin and gave her face to the sun.

There were several boats already anchored off the beach when they arrived. Children fought and screamed on rubber rafts, clam diggers waded in the shallows, early martinis glinted here and there. They anchored their boat next to Maynard Drogin's. Drogin appeared from inside his boat cabin attired in a skimpy black bathing suit. He was thin and incredibly white.

"Hey," he shouted, "get that thing out of here before somebody tries to land on it."

"Maynard, go below if you *have* a below on that tiny thing. Your body should never be seen by the public," George Potts yelled at him as he clinked around the bar.

Drogin rolled his eyes skyward. "It would seem that we cannot escape the vulgarities of life even here on the open water. Watch him, Christine. The man has been known to use his guests as galley slaves in drunken fits of pique."

Christine smiled. She liked these two absurd neighbors of hers. "If you two suburban sailors would pay less attention to insults," she said, "and more attention to seamanship, I'd feel a lot safer." She looked down at Nick. He was still talking with the two women, but his attention was focused on a boat anchored near them. Christine followed his gaze to a white sailboat, its tall, aluminum mast swaying gently. On the deck, lounging in bikinied perfection, her body stretched to the sun, was Karla Anderson. Nick was right, she thought. Too many serpents in Paradise. "Okay," she said. "Okay, captain. I'm going down below to put on this very tiny bikini I have." I shall fight fire with, as they say, fire, she thought. "Do you think you could make a pitcher of martinis by the time I come back?"

"Your wish is my command," Potts said, jiggling his hat comically.

Several minutes later she emerged onto the deck into the bright sunlight. Joey and his father were busily donning their snorkeling fins. Nick's arm went around his son's shoulder. "Hey, little pal," he said, "we haven't done very much together in the last few weeks, have we? We've got to change that, buddy. Pronto. Is it a deal?" Christine's face flushed with pleasure as she saw the slow smile spreading across Joey's face. After a moment, he said, "That's okay with me, Dad."

Nick tousled his son's hair. "And why, kiddo, do you want to spend more time with old Dad?"

Joey recognized the familiar tone, their game. "Because you're the best dad in the whole world." He waited patiently for Nick's response.

"That's only because I have the best son in the whole

wide world to play with." Nick's face became suddenly pained. He turned his head away.

Later that morning, Nick took a long swim with Christine. When they returned to the boat, he splashed her playfully as she went up the deck ladder. My God, Christine thought, that's the first time in weeks I've heard my husband laugh. I'm almost happy. Either the pieces of my life are coming together again or I shouldn't drink martinis in the morning.

By midafternoon everyone had gathered on the beach. It was a long, curving strand of brown sand and pebbles. Huge boulders were strewn among the waving sea grass. Charcoal grills appeared, followed by corn, lobsters, clams, and buckets of ice filled with cans of beer. Christine carefully avoided any contact with Karla Anderson. She felt too good for any outdoor unpleasantness. It was Karl Anderson who sat down beside her as she watched the clams simmer on the grill. He was immaculately dressed in white pants and shirt and a black blazer jacket. His great size always terrified her a little.

"You're looking well, Mrs. Marino," he said.

"Do you know, Mr. Anderson, that's the nicest thing you have ever said to me." Christine looked directly into the ice blue eyes.

"It is my curse to be perpetually misunderstood," he said. "I am really a wonderful person. Superior, actually. In some circles, I'm a prince. A true prince. Look, Mrs. Marino, the sun is shining, the cool waters invite, all animals are at rest. Let us, too, in Nature's peaceable kingdom, declare a truce. Let love and toleration be our password. My love, your toleration."

Christine looked at the big man. The martinis stirred pleasantly in her head. "I am not a rabbit, Mr. Anderson," she said.

"Understood. Understood."

"We are neighbors, you and I. No more hot hands on my body. No more allusions to romance to come, no more horny bullshit. Agreed?"

"Agreed. Reluctantly agreed." He grasped her hand impulsively. "Let us shake hands on it like two sane suburbanites." He leaned over her hand suddenly and kissed it. Christine stared down at the back of the huge neck matted with gold silver curls. When he lifted his head, the blue eyes struck her like an Arctic wind.

"What is it?" he said quietly.

Christine closed her eyes and shook her head. "It's nothing. Nice to make your acquaintance, Mr. Anderson. By the way, I hear that your mother is not feeling well. My husband is absolutely desolated."

"Ah, yes." The enigmatic smile again. "Poor mama is not herself today." He stared at her another moment and then turned suddenly away.

As Anderson's huge bulk passed in front of Christine, she saw that Bowen Stirner had been looking at the two of them. He smiled pleasantly as Christine waved to him. As always, when he looked at her, there was something in his eyes that his face did not show, an enigmatic depth that puzzled Christine, made her uncomfortable. The tanned girl on Stirner's arm shot a quick, questioning glance at Christine. Time to find my husband, Christine thought. She rose and walked down the beach toward Nick and Joey.

After lunch, the heat of the day brought activities to a standstill. A few children swam, someone played a song on a harmonica. George Potts stood up, staggering under a load of martinis. "My God," he said. "You people are *boring*. Let's *do* something. Let's bury Maynard in the sand and have a treasure hunt."

"No," Kimberly Potts said, pulling her husband down. "We did that last year. Nobody looked."

"How about a touch football game?" one of the teenagers suggested.

"Too hot," Potts answered. "Too many old fogeys." He seemed suddenly struck by an inspiration. "Wait! I've got it. We're going to have a talent show. It's all coming to me now. The Mill Harbor Follies. There must be loads of talent out there." He was on his feet again, waving his hands expansively toward the people seated around him. He was getting visibly drunker as he spoke. "Gather 'round, folks, gather 'round. Okay, okay, who's going to be first? Who wants to start us off?" There was a shaking of heads and much nervous laughter.

Maynard Drogin wavered unsteadily to his feet, a drink in his hand. "I can tap dance," he announced.

George Potts looked at him incredulously. "In bare feet? On sand? Sit down, Maynard." He made an ineffectual grab at the other man's arm, but Drogin tapped clumsily away, out of his reach, spilling most of his drink in the process. He was humming to himself now as he stared intently down at his feet. He collapsed ten seconds later amid scattered applause and loud hissing.

Potts looked down at the disheveled figure. "You show incredible promise, Maynard. Truly incredible. All right, folks, a really great start. Now who's going to be next? How about this lovely lady, right here?" He had stopped in front of Henrietta. To Christine's surprise, her aunt rose heavily to her feet, adjusted her wig, and stepped forward. After waiting for silence, she began to sing "Ten Cents a Dance" in a throaty voice with mild hip gyrations. Christine was embarrassed but when her aunt sat down she joined the others in their enthusiastic applause. Henrietta was followed by a large lady who sang "Because" in a mediocre voice. Someone recited a risqué version of "Trees," and Bowen Stirner recited Hamlet's soliloquy in Spanish.

A little girl, propelled by an unseen hand, walked into the center of the gathered people and proceeded to sing every song from the movie version of *The Wizard of Oz*. As Christine looked with amusement at the small, tanned figure, her eyes flared suddenly. Unnoticed by her, Karla Anderson had placed herself directly across the circle from where she and Nick were sitting. The girl was leaning back on a large boulder, the sun glinting off her bronzed limbs and golden hair. She had placed her guitar on the rock at her back and was staring at a spot in the sand directly in front of Nick. Christine looked casually at her husband. His face had that strange, clouded look she had grown to fear. He was staring at the same spot as the girl in a tense, brooding manner. Christine could sense the contact between them. It was as if they were staring deep into each other's eyes. She placed her hand tentatively on Nick's shoulder. He trembled slightly but did not otherwise acknowledge her presence. Hurt and puzzled, Christine withdrew her hand. Oh, God, she told herself, don't let it begin again. Don't let this day be spoiled. Don't let her spoil my life. She finished her martini and poured herself another. You're doing splendidly, she thought. Meet crisis with alcohol. Wonderful. She raised her glass to the girl and smiled. Here's looking at you, goddess. And to hell with you, neighbor.

Christine's hurt, defiant gaze found Bowen Stirner in the circle of faces around her. He was looking at Nick and Karla with rapt concentration, the pipe smoke floating lazily upward in front of him. After several moments he glanced at her. This time she did not look away. Stirner's face was a smoke-shrouded mask. Only his eyes revealed the intensity of his thoughts. Christine flung her head backward, letting her long hair cascade down alongside her face. Their eyes held.

After the little girl had retreated to sporadic applause, Christine was startled to see George Potts standing in front of her. "Come on, beautiful, how about it?" he said. "If you can't sing, just stand there and turn around slowly."

Christine shook her head and tried to wave him away. "No, George, go away. I am completely untalented. I . . ." As she spoke, her eyes caught the quick upward glance of the girl in front of her. Once again she saw that deep, burning hatred radiating from the implacable features. Without knowing why, Christine stood up. There were cheers and whistles from the onlookers. "Does anyone have a hat?" she said. A straw hat sailed out toward her from the crowd. Christine caught it in midair. More cheers and whistles. Placing it at a slant on her head, she raised her hands in front of her, palms outward, and started to sing:

Yes, sir, that's our Westport,
No sir, not South Norwalk,
Yes sir, that's our Westport High.

She accompanied herself with a few mechanical hand movements, and several halfhearted kicks. This is terrible, she thought. I mean, really terrible. If I haven't lost my husband before this, this should do the trick. She wondered vaguely how many drinks she had drunk as she continued through the rest of the cheer. After forgetting some key words, losing her balance once and her hat twice, she finally came to the end, shaking her head apologetically as she sat down. Christine wanted to sink into the sand until Joey came over and hugged her.

"Hey, Mom, that was great!" he said. Christine returned his hug as if she would never let him go.

"A beautiful performance by a beautiful woman." It was Potts again. "You are a vision, a true vision. Now, is there anyone else?" He turned around in the silence.

"Surely there must be some more talented people out there."

As he turned unsteadily on his feet, Karla Anderson's soft voice said, "I'd like to recite something . . . an old poem."

Potts bowed to her. "Ah, the absent Anderson. Where have you been all my life, dear creature?" He threw a few inebriate kisses in her direction and took several steps toward her. The girl did not speak or move, but Potts stopped in midstride, a peculiar look on his face. He threw two more halfhearted kisses and retreated to the edge of the audience. Karla Anderson adjusted the guitar on her shoulders and strummed it delicately. A pure, wordless singing issued from her mouth and drifted among the listeners. Small children who had been digging in the sand a moment before stopped and turned their heads toward her, their tiny shovels gripped in their hands. Every member of the audience was turned toward her rapt, unmoving. Only Bowen Stirner's face was different. As he glanced around at the silent onlookers, alarm came to his eyes, a tension straightened his mouth.

Despite herself, Christine was awed by the magic of the girl's voice, the beauty of the strange melody. Unwillingly, she looked up at the singer. The ice blue eyes were staring directly at Nick. Christine glanced at her husband. He was looking down at the sand in front of him like a pouting, unwilling child. Then, slowly, inexorably, as if he could not help himself, he raised his head until his eyes were locked with the girl's in deep, secret embrace. An alien embrace that was not love, but promises. The notes gradually died away. Then, as the guitar continued to play, in a voice of sun-sparkled crystal, she began to speak:

Come, my love, O my companion,
Can you hear Pan pipes?
Do you hear that sweet, primeval fluting
From the land of untouched regions?

Can you bear rapture that echoes in still trees,
That falls like rain
And pierces the caressed flesh of earth?
Will you delve the heart of desire?
Will you dance the fearful melody?
Come with me.

My voice, which is your fatality,
Glides like blinding lightning
Across the electric sea.
Come with me. Beneath the palms,
My voice, that is your destiny, sings.
Come with me, come with me.

Taste with me the indescribable wine,
Behold the terrific face of Joy,
Place your silver lips upon my lips of gold,
Enter my ancient, golden kingdom.

O golden realm, O realm of beauty and terror,
Where love lies like a mist on the gleaming hills,
And the jewelled leaves tremble and fall
From a thunder unheard.

O golden realm, O region of red delight,
Where the streams are scarlet running,
And each dark pool reveals
A smiling, crimson image.

O golden realm, O realm of ecstacy,
Where the plumed birds wheel
In the blood red night, O love,
Tonight, tonight
We shall drink from forbidden fountains.
Come with me.

Let us ride the back of the Dragon,
Pull down the moon and the stars;
Let us enter the infinite darkness,
And partake of violence divine.

For together, we can define the universe
With a secret smile to the forest,
A joyous yes to the night.

The voice stopped. The eyes of Nick and the girl
were fastened to each other with a look so intense it
might have been mistaken for anger, if it were not for
the slight smiles that creased their lips.

"That was lovely, dear," Kimberly Potts said, breaking the silence. "But, my dear, what on earth did you say?" The girl's attention remained unbroken. "Ah. It's a secret." Kimberly continued. "Okay. Bowen? Where are you? What did she say? What kind of poem was that?"

Bowen Stirner had not moved. He was regarding the girl through the smoke from his pipe.

"Bowen? What kind of poem was that?"

As if awakening from sleep, Bowen Stirner finally looked at her. After a long pause he said, "I want to phrase this very carefully, Kim." Another pause. "Let us say, if I had children, I would not recite it to them before bedtime." He rose suddenly and walked across the beach, staring out over the water.

"Aha," Kimberly Potts persisted. "I think the great intellectual is actually stumped." She turned to Anderson. "What do you know, Karl. I think your daughter has finally done it."

The huge man was peering thoughtfully at Bowen Stirner. Without turning his head, he said, "Yes, she has. She certainly has." After another moment, he lumbered heavily to his feet and looked around. "It looks as if the party's over, sailors. All survivors of the trip home are invited to the Andersons' for a final swim and several final drinks."

There were a few cheers. Nick stood up with the rest of the audience. His eyes had never left the girl's. "I'll be there," he said.

Christine's heart sank. "Nick, I'd rather not," she

said. "I think I've really had too much to drink already. And Joey and Henrietta must be tired."

Nick's eyes flicked toward her and back at the girl. "I'll be there," he repeated firmly. Then, pulling Joey along with him, he started toward the boat.

Anger surged through Christine. She looked coldly at Karla Anderson. The masked triumph she saw on the girl's face enraged her further. Then, as those ice blue eyes were slowly raised to meet hers, the venomous intensity she saw there hit Christine like a physical shock. Despite herself, she felt her anger turn into fear.

As she walked toward the Potts's dory, Christine noticed Bowen Stirner, still standing alone on the beach, gazing out over the water. He had not moved for several minutes. She walked over to him, touched his arm. "Bowen, what is it?"

He turned his head and looked searchingly into her eyes for a long moment. "Christine, I . . ." He stopped. His face looked like a reflection in a shattered mirror.

Christine reached for his hand. "What's the matter, Bowen? What's going on?"

"It's . . . nothing." He had collected himself quickly. "You'd better catch your boat, Chris."

Joey was waving at her from the dory. Christine waved back and started down the beach. What *is* going on? she thought. *What the hell is going on?*

One hour later, a robe over her bikini, Christine fretted about the kitchen, accomplishing nothing. Nick had gone to the Andersons', Joey and Henrietta were in the den watching television. She lit a cigarette and put it out immediately. You don't like to smoke, idiot, she told herself. She sat down. She stood up. She mixed herself a drink. At this rate you'll make Henrietta look like an amateur in no time, she thought. Damn Nick. Damn that bitch. She took a long drink. She thought about what a fool she had made of herself with her high school cheer. Damn all poetesses, she continued methodically. Damn all picnics. Damn all boats. "Damn sand." She stopped when she realized she had said the last two words out loud. "Okay," she said to the refrigerator, "I'm too drunk to cook and too sad to cry. So . . . everybody's going swimming, I'm going swimming." She picked up a large towel, waved at the television viewers who did not see her, and walked down to the beach.

The daylight was fading quickly. Christine spread the towel on the sand, took off her robe, and waded into the sun-crimsoned water. It felt cool and delicious on her skin. She plunged in, swam about for several minutes, and then emerged dripping and refreshed. She lay down on the towel, still wet, and looked up at the brightly lit clouds. Where had she heard it? The blood red sky. Beautiful. Why weren't people as beautiful as Nature was? Beautiful Nick. She reached behind her, unfastened her halter, and took it off. Nature girl, she thought. I don't need you, Nick. I'll live in the woods like Charlie Steinmetz. Bare-assed. Live on nuts and berries.

She heard steps behind her. Looking up, she saw

Attila padding down the path. When he reached her, he licked her knee once and then lay down heavily, his head on his paws. Christine put one hand on the powerful black shoulder. I've got plenty of friends, she thought. Nature friends. I'll be all right. She stared up at the slowly moving clouds that were graying now, her mind spinning down to reverie.

Two fighting blue jays drew Christine's attention to the dense vegetation behind her. The tall reeds waved gently, the willows silvered their leaves in the light evening breeze. The air was heavy with the scent of seaweed and flowers.

Deep among the rushes there was a dry rustling. A twig snapped. Attila's head was raised before the sound was gone. Drawing herself up on one elbow, Christine turned her head. "Zat you, Charlie?" she called. Hey, that's not funny, girl, she thought. What are you trying to do, scare yourself?

Beneath her hand, the dog rose slowly. A low growl started deep in his throat. Christine sat up, her halter pressed against her breasts. The dog was barking furiously now. She reached for his collar with her free hand.

"If there's anyone in there," she called out, her voice unsteady, "you'd better get the hell out of here. I don't know how long I can hold this dog." The animal was lunging madly now, wrenching Christine's arm with every leap. Then with one final effort he was free. In several bounds he had disappeared into the green undergrowth, barking fiercely. Christine stared after him in terrified fascination, unable to move.

The sound that split the evening air a moment later was an abomination. It was a single snarl, a roar. It came from the feral core of Nature itself; so savage, so voluminous that it defied reality. The ground beneath Christine trembled as, transfixed, she watched the sky fill with birds of every description, in silent, erratic flight.

As quickly as it came, it rumbled away. Silence flowed in like an incoming tide. Nothing moved, except the birds in their silent frenzy. Her eyes wide in naked terror, Christine waited for the dog to return. There was only silence. She saw that her hands were shaking. "Oh God, oh Mama," she heard herself whispering repeatedly. She sprang up, dropping her halter. Like an automaton, she began to run, looking back over her shoulder. She was crying now, saying the same words over and over again. Once inside the front door, she threw the bolt and leaned with her back against it. She kept repeating the words, her eyes closed.

Two uniformed policemen and Lieutenant Broderick arrived ten minutes after her call. The detective strode toward her quickly, his auburn hair and moustache glowing in the bright light, the green eyes shrewd and steady. His incisive manner comforted Christine. She knew she had been near hysteria.

"Mrs. Marino," he said, looking at her closely, "can you tell me again what happened? You sounded very upset on the telephone."

"My dog," Christine said. She could not stop the

tears. "I think he's . . . he's killed something. Down by the beach. I heard . . . I heard . . ."

"Okay. It's okay. Can you take us down to where it happened?"

Christine looked at the solid figures of the three men in front of her. "All right," she said. "All right. Let me get a coat." While she was tying her coat belt, Christine put her hand on the detective's arm. "Is it him, Lieutenant?" she said. "Is it Steinmetz again?"

"No, that's the first thing we checked. He's safely tucked away in Pilgrim State."

"Then who . . . then what . . ."

The detective strode past her. "Let's take a look and see, Mrs. Marino."

As they walked toward the corral, Christine heard voices and laughter. A group of revelers from the Andersons' was walking toward them along the shore. George Potts waved at her, drink in hand. "What's up, beautiful? We heard the sirens. Don't tell me we've got crazy visitors again." Christine looked for Nick, but he had not come with the others.

"Old Steinmetz." It was Karl Anderson. He stood there weaving from side to side. "One helluva guy." Christine saw Lieutenant Broderick look at him coldly.

She waited on the beach with the others as the three men converged on the heavily reeded area. They had unstrapped their holsters, hands resting lightly on their revolver butts. After what seemed an eternity to Christine, she heard Lieutenant Broderick utter a long string of oaths. She heard the sound of someone else retching. In another moment Broderick stepped out onto the beach, his face pale and subdued, his eyes like steel.

Christine stepped forward. "What is it, Lieutenant? What did he do?"

Lieutenant Broderick shook his head tiredly. "He didn't do anything, Mrs. Marino. Your dog is dead."

"Dead? What do you mean? How could . . ." She took a step toward the tall reeds. The detective raised his arms blocking her way.

"I tell you he's dead, Mrs. Marino. Don't go in there."

Christine looked at him, bewildered, angry. "Let me go," she said. Tears were in her eyes again. "Let me pass. That's my dog in there. I've got to take him home, bury him."

"Damnit, Mrs. Marino, you can't bury him." Christine's eyes grew wide. "You can't do it, damnit," he continued, his voice harsh with frustration. "He's been torn apart. There's nothing left of him."

Christine's eyes could not leave his face. As she began to comprehend the enormity of his words, fear drew her mouth into a square, made her face suddenly seem old.

Behind her, his hand waving drunkenly, Karl Anderson lifted a glass to the pale red sky. "Hail to the Beast," he said. "Bump in the night," he said. "The Beast, my friends, is back."

13

"You can't do it," Henrietta said. She took a long drink of the steaming coffee and closed one eye. "What could I possibly have drunk last night that would make everything look yellow?"

Christine looked at the dear, balding head, the tattered sweater over the nightgown, and said nothing.

"If you cut and run, if you leave, my dear brother will have a heredity hemorrhage in his grave."

"A what?"

"Honor. Heritage, girl. A Knapp does not run from danger. A Knapp conquers, prosecutes, and convicts danger."

"This Knapp-Marino is leaving," Christine said firmly. "I cannot conquer what's out there. Last night something horrible happened. There is something that kills out there. I have a son. I'm leaving."

"You also have a husband," Henrietta reminded her.

"Ha!"

"You have a husband who loves you and will protect you. Show some pride, Christine." Henrietta's voice had become serious, almost harsh.

Christine shook her head. "I've got pride, Henrietta. I love this place. I'm proud of what we've done here. But you, Auntie, did not hear what I heard. You didn't see those policemen's faces. What I lack is courage."

"Courage! Do what you have to do, sweetie. I heard that . . . thing. And I vote to stay right here."

Christine looked at the old, badly made-up face. There was a stubborn solidity there she wished she felt. "You're making me look bad, you know that, don't you," she said.

Henrietta nodded. "I'm trying, dearie," she replied.

Christine stood up and kissed her aunt lightly on the forehead. "We'll see," she said.

Bowen Stirner telephoned at four o'clock. Christine was surprised at how pleased she was to hear his voice.

"Chris," he said, "I heard what happened to you. You okay?"

"Sort of," Christine said.

"Listen, I've got to talk to you. Maximum agenda. First of all, do you have any cold beer? It's not for me, it's for my head and body. I'm detoxifying slowly."

"Yes, I do," Christine said.

"Good. That's why I love you. You have compassion. It should take me about twenty minutes to crawl over there."

Christine hung the receiver up and almost smiled as she watched Henrietta plod upstairs quickly toward wig and mascara.

Bowen Stirner stood in the doorway, framed by sunlight. God, Christine thought, he's hung over and he looks magnificent.

"You look terrible," she said. They smiled briefly at each other. They had shared something on the beach, some small empathy, and there was a closeness between them now that had not been there before. She seated him in the living room and returned a moment later with a cold beer and a hastily frosted glass.

"Bless you, my child," he said, taking a long drink. "You have just delayed an ugly display of delirium tremens."

Christine did not speak. She looked down at her knee, making little circles on it with her finger. She could feel him watching her as he took another drink.

"So?" he said finally.

"So." She did not look up.

After a moment, he said, "That was quite a day yesterday."

"Yes, it was," she replied quietly.

"Chris, I want to explain the way I acted on the beach. You caught me at rather a bad moment. A bad moment." He paused. The circles continued. "It was that girl. Karla." The circles stopped. "She upset me. She upset me very much."

Christine, remembering his face, said nothing.

"She's quite a good little singer. Quite good. Nice tone. Perfect pitch. I'd like to know who writes her stuff. And a poetess as well. My goodness, what a poetess. We'll have to get together sometime and discuss her work."

"You'll have to get in line." The circles started again. She could feel Stirner's eyes on her.

After a moment, he said, "Nick? I saw it last night. Is it bad?"

She finally looked up at him. "Bad? What's bad about your husband falling in love with a young, beautiful girl. It happens all the time. Go with the times, Bowen. Get with it, you stodgy old thing." She could feel the tears coming.

"Bad," he agreed.

Christine tossed her head in frustration.

"Is it bad if in your own backyard your dog, which should be able to kill almost anything on this earth, gets torn apart as if by some cruel idiot torturing an insect? Is it bad if your husband is out screwing his poetess instead of being home protecting his son and his wife?" She swallowed hard. "It's bad, Bowen. It's bad." Her face crumpled suddenly. She put a hand on her forehead. "It's bloody, fucking awful." The tears came.

Stirner watched her, saying nothing. He sipped his beer. When she had stopped crying, he wordlessly offered her a handkerchief.

Christine wiped her eyes, touched her hair. "I must look a mess," she said, trying to smile.

His stare was straight, compassionate. "No," he said finally, "you don't look a mess, Christine."

Henrietta swept into the living room. She had on a long dress with roses sewn all over it and the huge wig festooned with a thousand blond ringlets. Her arms, wrists, and throat jangled with jewelry of every description. The air was filled with heavy, medium-priced perfume.

"Dr. Stirner! What a truly pleasant surprise," she said. "I was just on my way to the veranda for my one, tiny afternoon aperitif. *Pour* the circulation, *n'est-ce pas?* I insist that you join me. Now, don't say *non.*" She looked at Christine. "And you, too, dearie. You look like hell. Now, I'll just go and get the glasses and the gin and wait for you to finish your little *tête-à-tète* here. Don't be too long, *ma petite. Au revoir* for now." She tapped him on the head with her glasses and flowed out of the room.

Bowen Stirner stared after her steadily, rubbing his forehead. "It must be wonderful to be bilingual like that," he commented.

"Yes, we're very proud of her." The flicker of a smile played at the corners of Christine's mouth, then died away. There was a short silence. "Bowen, what am I going to do? I'm terrified. I was thinking of leaving. Packing up and getting out of here. It would solve . . . so many problems."

Stirner poured the last of the beer into the glass. "You can't do that, Christine. This is not the first time something like this has happened around here. We didn't run away. You can't do it."

"Maybe you should have run. All of you. Bowen, how do you think I bought this house? Someone, something frightened the Levines. They ran like hell."

"Yes, I remember," Stirner's eyes narrowed.

"There's something out there. Something . . . unnatural. It must be . . . to do things like that."

"Perhaps." Stirner stared at her, not seeing her. "Perhaps. Or maybe it's the other way around."

"I don't understand, Bowen."

"You and I, Christine, Man, we're the unnatural ones. We have our laws, we build our cities, we rise above, we cherish our artifacts, we play our little games. Our fierce friend out there, he's the natural one, he's closest to the earth. Raw, powerful, pitiless. He plays no games. No sportsman he."

"I have a small son, Bowen."

"Stay here, Chris. There are police all over Mill Harbor. They'll find him."

Christine shook her head. "They haven't yet."

Stirner drummed his fingers on the back of the couch. He seemed to be deciding something. After a long moment he spoke. "Then *we'll* do it."

"What?"

"We'll find him. You and I."

"Are you out of your mind? A, I'm leaving. B, I'm a coward. I mean a real, no-fooling-around coward. C, my family life is going up in smoke, which causes me, D, to think in terms of suicide. And you want me to go stalking around in the bulrushes looking for . . . for God knows what. You must be joking."

"I'm not joking."

"Let the police handle it, Bowen."

"They're doing what they can. I think we're dealing here with something . . . beyond their understanding. All you really have to do is one thing. I'd do it myself, but I'm going to be buried in libraries for the next few days."

"Forget it."

"I want you," he said, looking directly at her, "to pay a visit to the Levines. Tomorrow, if possible. They live in Connecticut. I'll phone you their address in the morning. I want you to talk to Mrs. Levine. See if you can talk to her daughter, Jill. Remember everything they say. Everything. Write it down if you have to. Will you do it?"

"Drive to Connecticut?"

"Will you do it, Christine?"

"No, I can't leave . . ."

The sound of tires came from the driveway. Christine tensed, stopped speaking. In another moment the front door slammed and Nick was standing in the entrance to the living room. His face looked puffy, almost bloated. His hair clung wetly to his forehead. There were streaks of mud on his clothes.

"Dr. Stirner, I presume," Nick said, his voice thick and hoarse.

Bowen Stirner observed the other man closely. He stared at his face for several long seconds before he spoke. "Nick, how are you? You look just wonderful."

"Bad night," Nick said. "Woke up in their boathouse at ten o'clock this morning. Must've passed out. Had a wonderful day, too. Had an argument with my brother, Alfredo. Decked him with a fucking chair. My father threw me out of the restaurant. I think I bit his thumb half off. And now I come home and I find you two," he raised his voice to a shout, "cozy as hell."

Christine looked at Nick, barely believing what she saw and heard. His description of what he had done appalled her. Even more disturbing was his physical appearance. She hardly recognized him. The matted, unkempt hair, the yellowed teeth behind the unfamiliar set of his mouth, the eyes that held a wildness she had never seen before. And there was a coarseness about him that shocked her most of all. In the way he moved and spoke, in the thickened waist and neck. My God, she thought. I hardly recognize him anymore.

"Ahh, forget it, Doc," Nick said loudly. "Just my little joke. I trust you, Doc. Have a drink."

Stirner stood up. "I don't think so, Nick," he said. "Thanks anyway, but I've got to go. Maybe you should skip it, too, pal. Say, how much weight have you put on recently? Twenty, thirty pounds? You're getting fat." He waited intently for Nick's answer.

"Yeah, about that." Nick smiled. "Big and mean, baby, big and mean."

Stirner's eyes were looking at the other man's face and neck. "How about going jogging with me some morning, getting rid of that flab, my friend."

Nick walked in front of Stirner. His mouth was still smiling but there was no mirth there. His eyes gleamed. "Jog, my ass, friend," he said. He poked the taller man's shoulder twice with his forefinger in a slow, deliberate manner. Then he turned, left the room, and went up the stairs.

Christine stood up. "I'm sorry, Bowen. I don't know what to say."

Stirner's eyes were following Nick on the stairway. "It's all right," he said abstractedly. "It's all right." He turned and faced Christine. "Will you do that for me tomorrow, Chris? You must." His eyes went back to the stairs. "It's very important."

Christine nodded once. As she accompanied him to the door, Henrietta came into the living room from the terrace. Her right hand was artfully at her throat. "Where *is* everyone," she said. "Time flies, ice melts. Those are the only two *certainements* of life. All else is mirage, it is . . ." She saw Stirner leave through the front door. Her fingertips still at her throat, she stared after him. "Oh, shit," she said.

Later that evening, the doorbell rang. Christine was surprised and delighted to see Sal Valenti and three of Nick's other friends from the old neighborhood standing there. She had completely forgotten that they were coming. Throwing her arms around the stocky man warmly, Christine said, "Oh, Sal, it's so good to see you. Nick will be surprised. You couldn't have come at a better time."

They walked into the living room arm in arm. Sal looked around at the spacious room. "Eh, Chris, that *paisan* husband of yours is stealing from his father like I told him. It's nice but the crickets would drive me crazy. At least cockroaches are quiet."

"All you guys were crazy," Christine said. "And I see you haven't changed. I really don't know why I like you so much."

Nick appeared in the doorway to the living room. His eyes widened. He seemed to be struggling to remember something. Then his face clouded over with anger. "What the hell are you guys doing here?" he asked flatly.

His tone brought an awkward silence to the room. After several moments, during which Sal appraised Nick's appearance with amazement, he walked over and threw his arms around his impassive host.

"Nicky, Nicky. Always the kidder. How you been, pally? You look terrible. How much weight you put on? You ain't my lean and mean Nicky no more."

Christine came over and took Nick's arm. "Nick, isn't this a wonderful surprise? I thought it would be a great idea for you and the boys to get together again."

Nick looked at her expressionlessly. "You did?"

Christine was taken aback. Something's wrong, she thought. This is not working out.

"These city rats don't look comfortable away from a bar. Why don't you guys go out and talk over old times," she suggested hopefully.

Sal waved his hand negatively and looked at Nick. "I hear all you got out here in the suburbs is cocktail lounges. I ain't going to no cocktail lounge. You got any bars around here?"

Nick did not reply. Sal glanced at his friends questioningly. They shrugged their shoulders.

"There are a couple of bars almost sleazy enough for

you guys just off the main road," Christine broke in desperately. "Nick knows where they are. Come on, honey. Show them the seedier side of Mill Harbor."

She watched as a reluctant Nick and his four friends got into Sal's dented Cadillac. She shut the door and leaned against it, her eyes closed in silent prayer.

They returned within an hour.

When she heard the car in the driveway, Christine's heart sank in dismay. She rushed from the bedroom. As she descended the stairs, Nick brushed past her.

"What happened, honey?" she said. "Why are you back so soon?"

Nick did not even turn around.

Christine continued down the stairs and hurried out into the driveway. Sal was standing by the open door of the car, its motor running. He was looking up at the bedroom window, a puzzled and angry look on his face.

"Sal, what is it?" Christine asked anxiously. "What happened?"

Sal's eyes remained on the window. "Your husband is a real weirdo, Chris. He needs help."

"Tell me, Sal, what happened? What did Nick do?"

His gaze slowly left the window and his eyes stared deeply into her own. He started to say something but stopped himself. "Forget it, Chris," he finally said. "But I'll tell you this: that ain't the Nicky I used to know." He turned suddenly, got into the car, and sped off down the driveway.

Christine stood there hugging herself, shivering in the warm night air.

14

As Christine drove across the Throgs Neck Bridge toward Connecticut, to her right she could see Long Island emerging from the morning fog, the Merchant Marine Academy at Kings Point just starting to appear. On her left the towers of Manhattan pierced through the heated miasma that covered the city like the spires of some half-remembered, mythical kingdom.

Christine's mind could not dispel the fears that the previous night had raised. The look on Sal's face, his reticence, still haunted her. She had thought of insisting that Nick tell her what had happened, but she did not. She was afraid of what she might discover. And here I am, she thought, about to pry into the lives of total strangers.

What am I doing here? Why am I doing this? There had been something in Bowen Stirner's face yesterday, in the tone of his voice, the way he had looked at Nick. He knew something. And if he was on to something that would stop this nightmare, she had to help.

The air conditioning and soft music soothed her. It was pleasant to be away from her house of troubles, from Nick. She had looked at his face for a long time that morning as he slept. She did not like what she saw. Aside from the thickening of his features, his unaccustomed lack of grooming, there was something else. A loss of laughter, an indefinable brutality that had never been a part of Nick before.

She had spoken to Loreto Marino early that morning. His hand was bandaged and Alfredo had five stitches in the back of his scalp. Loreto had said that he understood, but Christine could hear in his voice that he did not. She had never known anything but a tough gentleness from her father-in-law and she was shocked by the depths of his anger. They had both agreed that Nick had to go to a psychiatrist as soon as possible.

She passed quickly through Westchester County and entered Connecticut at Greenwich. By ten o'clock, she had found the correct exit for Madison. Mrs. Levine had reluctantly agreed to wait for her until eleven. Twenty minutes later she pulled into the driveway of an old frame house with exterior porches all around the first floor and an extensive lawn, dotted here and there with tall maple trees. She rang the bell.

Sandra Levine must have been a good-looking woman in her time, Christine thought, but this was not her time. The blond hair, hurriedly combed, had long black roots. There were dark circles under her eyes. The skin over her cheekbones was drawn and waxen. Veins pulsed at her temples and throat. Beneath the white slacks and tan blouse, the body was too thin, the posture weary.

They sat in the living room. There was no coffee, no small talk.

"I'm not quite sure, Mrs. Marino, why you phoned me, why you're here. The fact that your dog was killed is a police matter. What does it have to do with me?" The husky voice was well modulated.

The woman's eyes bothered Christine. They were humorless, defeated. "It was good of you to see me, Mrs. Levine," she said. "I just thought you might be able to . . . help me in some way."

"Help you? I don't know what you mean."

"Both of my dogs," Christine continued, "were killed in a very terrible manner. In a single instant something destroyed them, tore them apart." Christine saw the other woman's body stiffen slightly, the eyes flare with emotion. "I understand you had some pet trouble, too, and I was wondering, Mrs. Levine, if you could tell me about it."

The woman stared into a corner of the room for a long time. She turned and faced Christine. "Get out of that house, Mrs. Marino," she said.

"What? I don't . . ."

"Get out," Mrs. Levine repeated in a low voice. "Leave that house. Sell it and get out."

"You can't really be serious," Christine said. The intensity of the woman's voice startled her.

"Mrs. Marino, look at me." The voice was softer now. "Do you think I've always looked like this? Do you think I've always acted this way? Do you know that I used to actually laugh? Living in that house destroyed me, Mrs. Marino, because it destroyed my daughter. Why do you think I've spoken to you the way I have, acted the way I have? I felt guilty about selling you, or anyone, that house. That house, that whole neighborhood, there's something evil there, something . . ." She stopped.

"I don't understand what . . ."

"Can you understand," the other woman interrupted, her voice rising, "that there is something unspeakable in Mill Harbor, something vile, something that kills. Get out of that house, Mrs. Marino, and run."

Christine, looking at the eyes of the distraught woman in front of her, felt the familiar fears burst forth from where she had hidden them, rampant, myriad, like the buds of some poisonous plant. It was with an effort that she controlled her voice. "I can't run without sufficient reason, Mrs. Levine. Tell me what you know. Then I can make a decision."

Mrs. Levine shook her head. "The police asked me never to discuss it. I'd like to help you, but I'm not going through that again. I can't."

"I can." A thin teenaged girl stood at the entrance to the living room. She was dressed in blue jeans, a white blouse, and moccasins. Her long brown hair hung down in front of her shoulders, framing a pretty, pale face. The blue circles under her eyes made her look older, haunted somehow.

"Jill! Jill, honey. Mrs. Marino and I are having sort of a private conversation. Shouldn't you be resting, dear?"

"Mother," the girl said patiently, "I've been sitting on the steps. I know what you're talking about." Her voice sounded tired, like an old woman's. She turned to Christine, but did not come into the room. "I don't care what the police say, Mrs. Marino. I'll tell you anything you want to know."

"Well, Jill," Christine began gently, "I guess you heard. Both my dogs were killed by something. I know you had some . . . trouble of your own . . . had a pet . . . killed."

Mrs. Levine stood up abruptly. "Mrs. Marino," she said, "I'm sorry you came here. You have no right to bring this all up again, to upset my daughter."

"It's all right, Mother. Dr. Braun says I *should* talk about it." She turned to Christine. "I've just spent five months in a mental hospital, Mrs. Marino. For four of those months I could not talk at all. Catatonic. From shock. I'm still in therapy. Without my pills you wouldn't want to know me. I can't go to school yet. I can't even leave the house without shaking."

Christine was looking down at the polished wooden floor. She could feel Mrs. Levine's eyes on her but she did not look up.

"I woke up one morning last March, Mrs. Marino, and went down to the corral before breakfast. I had a pet horse. Brandy. I used to like to talk to him in the mornings, feed him, water him, maybe take a short ride. He was a good friend of mine." After a pause, she continued. "What I found . . . what I found . . ." The girl swallowed, struggled to continue. "One of his hind legs had been torn off his body. It was just . . . lying there in the corral. The police said that's how he died. Ripped apart. Just like your dog."

A wave of pure terror went through Christine like an electric shock. She found it difficult to breathe.

"I got hysterical, they tell me, when I saw this and just started to run around, looking for . . . the rest of him. I guess I was screaming. I finally found him. In the Andersons' boathouse. He was hanging up by his . . . his one hind leg. His head had been twisted off. I . . . I saw it lying in the corner. His body looked funny, like it had shrunk. The police said . . ."

"Jill!" It was Mrs. Levine.

"The police told my parents that something had . . . had drunk the blood out of its body. I heard them." Her voice trailed off. The frightened eyes were staring at nothing out of the pale face.

Christine sat mute, unmoving. This isn't true, she thought, this can't be happening. She saw a small boy playing in the corral, sunlight on his dark hair.

Joey, she thought.

Run, she thought, run.

15

hristine was playing badminton with Joey when Bowen Stirner's car drove up the next morning. As he walked toward them in his yellow slacks and white shirt Christine realized how glad she was to see him. He had become a friend whose support she had begun to need.

"Hi, sport," he said to Joey, "Who's winning?"

"I am. She's terrible. You want to play?"

"I will, sport, if you'll let me borrow your mom for ten minutes."

As Christine walked toward the terrace with Stirner,

she turned suddenly. "Play right here where I can see you, Joey." There was a strident urgency in her voice that did not escape the man beside her.

When they were seated, Bowen Stirner leaned forward eagerly. "Well?" he said. "Did you see Mrs. Levine? Did she tell you anything?"

"I spoke to the daughter, Bowen. She told me everything. I'm frightened, Bowen. I can't stay here. Not now."

He waved his hand impatiently. The gray eyes glittered with excitement. "Tell me everything, Chris. Leave out nothing."

Christine found it difficult to talk. She composed herself with an effort. "The daughter, Jill, had a pet horse. It died. It died because someone, something, pulled one of its hind legs off."

Stirner's eyes grew wide and blinked several times. "My God, Christine, do you realize what you're saying? The mind and body that could conceive and carry out an act like that . . ."

"There's more, Bowen. After the horse was killed, it was hung up in the Andersons' boathouse. And then . . . and then something twisted its head off and sucked the blood out of the body . . ." Christine stared at Bowen Stirner helplessly. She found no haven in the fierce eyes. She found fear, and the beginning of a terrible understanding.

"My God," he said. "It fits. I can't believe this. Oh God, it fits."

"What fits? What is it, Bowen?" He continued to

stare into space, shaking his head in disbelief. "Bowen!" Christine's hand was on his shoulder. "Tell me!"

"I'm sorry, Christine. It would be foolish of me to tell you what I'm thinking. Let's say it's not a logical explanation. I have to research it more, sort it out. Do you think you can get that detective, what's his name, Broderick, here on Friday, around noon?"

"I'll try, Bowen," Christine said, "but you can't just . . ."

"I have to." He took hold of one of her fingers gently. "Don't you know, Christine, that the good always emerge victorious?" His smile was forced, the eyes unfathomable.

Christine did not smile back. "I'd like a guarantee, Bowen," she said.

He glanced at her quickly and then looked away. Christine watched as he forced his mouth into a smile again. "I think I shall now get up," he said, "and beat the pants off your son."

Christine watched him stride across the lawn. Why don't you sort out your own research, lady, she thought. A, I'm scared more than ever. B, I want to move. C, the good doctor knows something I'm not sure I want to hear. D, whatever it is he knows has frightened him. Christine had seen it that day on the beach, and today she had seen it again. Masked, fleeting, but unquestionable. The good doctor was afraid. Nick, terrible, wonderful Nick. He was not afraid of anything on earth. Nick's psyche was carved in granite, his body an arrow. Night things did not fool with Nick. She longed to confide in him now, to hide in his strength.

That evening, Christine sat alone with Nick in the living room. She was pretending to read a book while Nick sat staring at nothing. Christine waited. After half an hour of silence, it began. Nick rolled up his shirt sleeves and wiped his forehead repeatedly. Christine knew the routine by heart now.

"Boy, it's hot," he said. Christine did not look up. "Humid, too." Christine didn't know whether to smile or cry. Nick stood up. "I think I'll go over to the Andersons' for a quick swim. Want to come?" Christine shook her head slightly. Nick was standing in front of her. She sensed his eyes on her face. A long pause. "I could stay here," he said finally. "It's been a long time, Chris." They had not made love for several weeks, since Nick had attacked her in the bathroom.

Christine looked up at him steadily. She remembered her head forced into the sink, her wrist in a vicelike grip. "I don't want to make love with you, Nick," she said. "It hurts my arms."

He flinched visibly. "I've told you I was sorry about that. How many times can I say I'm sorry?"

Christine's eyes were back on the book. "I was wondering about that myself, Nick. It seems I'm hearing that word a lot around here lately." She couldn't even see the words now. There were tears in her eyes. Damn, she thought.

Nick stood there without moving. After a long moment, she raised her eyes to his defiantly. The expression on his face was so strange that Christine forgot her anger, could only stare. They remained that way, staring at one another, locked in pain. He stretched one hand tentatively toward her.

"Good-bye, my love," he whispered softly. He did not touch her. He turned and left the room.

Christine sat there unmoving. The tears flowed down her cheeks freely. She had seen something in the bedlam of her husband's eyes. What was it? Helplessness? A type of drowning? She remembered his outstretched hand. I'm tired, she thought. I'm very tired. She stood up, the book slipping unnoticed to the floor.

Christine lay in bed, her eyes dry now, the expression in them a sadness beyond tears. She stared at the full moon through the bedroom window. Thick summer clouds hung motionless in the sky, their summits coppered by the moonlight. The smell of lilac came drifting through the open window. This place, this house, was Eden until the serpents came, she thought. Damn the serpents.

A sudden breeze fluttered the curtains. It brought with it an unnatural, eerie sound. It was the soft howling that Christine had heard weeks ago coming from the Anderson boathouse. It ululated in the night, rising and falling in mystical harmony. Christine shivered. Dogs, she thought. Or beasts. The serpents are among us.

16

There are the doughnuts? You said if I came here at noon, Friday, there would be coffee *and* doughnuts. I don't see the doughnuts, Mrs. Marino."

Christine looked into the hard eyes of Lieutenant Broderick, at his unsmiling mouth. She knew he was joking, but she was never quite sure with him. "I thought policemen had to abstain while on duty," she said.

"Ah, yes," he said. The direct gaze caught her off guard. "Pity." Christine liked the way he looked at her. It was not suggestive. It was with admiration. "I think that's the professor's car," he said. "What he has to say had better be pretty interesting. I gave up raiding a porno movie for this."

Christine shook her head in mock disapproval and poured him another cup of coffee.

Bowen Stirner strode into the room purposefully. He had dressed in a blue blazer, gray slacks and shirt, and a maroon tie. He carried a large briefcase with him. He looks like a lawyer about to present a case, Christine thought.

After the coffee was finished, Lieutenant Broderick leaned back in his chair and lit a cigarette. "Now, Professor," he said, "I am officially on duty. What have you got for me?"

Stirner glanced at him. His manner was agitated, eager. He rose suddenly and walked over to the bay window, staring out of it, his hands clasped behind his back. "How are you coming on the killing of those two teenagers, Lieutenant?" he asked.

Broderick's eyes became serious. "We're working on it, Dr. Stirner," he said. "We're doing what has to be done."

"It wasn't Steinmetz, was it, Lieutenant?" Stirner's eyes had not moved from the window.

"We're not ruling anyone out yet, Doctor. Steinmetz, nor anyone else."

"It wasn't Steinmetz," Stirner repeated evenly. "We both know that. He couldn't have done that to a car."

Broderick's body tensed. "What about the car?" His voice was low.

"Lieutenant, Mrs. Marino and I both know what happened to them. It wasn't Steinmetz, and you know it."

Broderick waited, saying nothing.

"The Levines' horse, Lieutenant," Stirner continued. "Did you ever find out who killed it?"

Broderick looked surprised but did not answer.

"We also know the manner in which that horse died, Lieutenant. Mrs. Marino visited the Levines. Now this last incident, Mrs. Marino's dog. We all were there, Lieutenant. We know how that dog died." He raised his head, his eyes closed. "If I were in police work, Lieutenant, I would begin to notice things."

Broderick's voice was hard and flat. "I'm in police work," he said. "What's on your mind?"

"The similarities, Lieutenant. The congruencies. A history of pet decapitation here in Mill Harbor. Mrs. Marino's first dog. Decapitated. Those two teenagers. You were *there*, Lieutenant. You *saw* it. Then Mrs. Marino's other dog. Decapitated. Decimated. All these incidents, Lieutenant. These deeds. These," his voice rose sharply, "massacres! All these acts of violence, each exhibiting a savagery and a physical strength almost beyond our comprehension. Has it ever struck you, Lieutenant, that all these acts of horror were the work of one person?"

"It crossed my mind, yes."

Stirner turned and faced them. "What would you do, Lieutenant, if I told you that I think I know why these acts were committed and who committed them?"

"I'd listen," Broderick said, stroking his moustache thoughtfully.

Christine, listening to both men, sensed a mild antagonism between them, a fencing. Bowen was being dramatic, of course, but he was on to something. She could feel it.

"I have a problem," Stirner continued. "A credibility problem. In your work, Lieutenant, you deal in facts, circumstantial evidence, motive. My facts are mythic, my evidence no longer exists, and my motive is metaphysical. Do you follow me?"

"I follow you." Broderick lit another cigarette.

Stirner looked at him quickly and smiled. "Let us use an example. Suppose I told you that vampires exist. If I gave you sufficient proof, could you believe it?"

"Could I believe that there are abnormal people who like to drink blood, yes. We have one of them on file in this county. If you mean someone who can change into a bat and all that other jazz, then you would indeed have a problem."

"But with sufficient proof, *could* you believe it?" Stirner persisted.

Broderick exhaled a large cloud of smoke slowly. "With difficulty. With great difficulty, Professor. Is that our problem, a vampire?"

"No. A vampire is a cream puff compared to our boy here. Every living thing on earth is a ladyfinger next to our boy. His lusts are as elemental as an earthquake. His physical power defies the imagination. It is the strength of giants. And yet he's human. The son of a bitch is mostly human."

The usual sardonic twist to Broderick's mouth was gone as he peered through the smoke at Stirner. "A human with the strength of a giant?"

Stirner shook his forefinger back and forth. *"Mostly* human, Lieutenant. An important fraction. A terrifying fraction. Because the rest of him is beast. Malevolent, murdering beast. A creature of nightmare, of archaic horrors. A descendant of primal darkness who dwells among us. An . . . offspring . . ."

Broderick waved his hand impatiently. "What have we got, Professor?"

"What we have, my friend, is a troll. A dyed-in-the-wool, nonmythological, slaughtering troll."

"A what?" Broderick's eyes narrowed.

"A troll, Lieutenant. The result of the union between a giant and a human."

Broderick leaned back, his fingers interlaced, his eyes skeptical. "Giants, Professor? Giants?"

Stirner stared down at the seated man. "I fully understand, Lieutenant, that in order to convince you of what we are dealing with here, I have to first convince you of the former existence of giants. No giants, no trolls. No trolls, no suspect. First, before I destroy an area of your belief system, let me state that I do not for an instant imply the existence of giants now or in the recent past. But thousands, perhaps millions of years ago there *were* giants on earth. These giants mated with humans and down through the eons their descendants have inhabited this earth." Stirner paused and regarded the other man.

"I'm listening," Broderick said.

Nodding slightly, Stirner continued. "My recent studies have been a revelation to me. Some of the greatest minds in history have written about, perhaps believed in, giants. Virgil, Ovid, Plutarch, Apollodorus, Hesiod, all wrote about them. Spenser, in the *Faerie Queene*, wrote about 'an hideous giant, horrible and hie, that with his talnesse seems to threat the skie'; Jonathan Swift had his Brobdingnagians in *Gulliver*; Milton, in *Paradise Lost*, describes Satan in terms of giant stature. Rabelais gave us Gargantua. In India there was Hidimba, a red-bearded man-eater. In Lapland, Stalo, who wore garments of iron; the Tartars gave us one-eyed Depeghoz.

"The entire culture and religion of the ancient Norsemen was based on giants. Large gentleman. The entire sky was the inside of the skull of Ymir, chief of Rimthursar. This evil race inhabited Chaos and would eventually pull down the Nordic gods from the skies in a monumental, final battle.

"The ancients made statues of giants everywhere. In Egypt, at Luxor and Karnac, the statues are over fifty feet high. Life-sized? In the Parthenon at Athens, the statue of Minerva stood thirty-six feet high. The Colossus of Rhodes is one of the seven wonders of the ancient world. Tell me why the statues on Easter Island stand fifteen feet tall? All over the Pacific, and in China and Japan, we find the ruins of statues of giant stature. Do sculptors all over the earth fantasize in precisely the same manner?

"You know what bothers me the most. The ancient Greeks. The beautiful, clearheaded, realistic ancient

Greeks. They believed in giants, too. Greek poets and historians thought their contemporaries were dwarfs compared to their ancestors. The heroes of the Trojan War were thought to be giants in size. Herodotus tells us that the shoe of Perseus, who slew the Medusa, measured one yard in length. Homer wrote of Polyphemus, the Cyclops, a one-eyed man-eater. Greek mythology is filled with tales of Titans, giants with fifty heads and a hundred arms, powerful enough to storm Olympus, the home of their gods."

Broderick put out his cigarette deliberately. "I deal in proof, Professor. Evidence. Not mythology."

Stirner's eyes flashed. "I have predicted what you would say, Lieutenant, and I am prepared. Let us discuss evidence. In 1712, a certain Dr. Mather found and recorded the discovery of a human thighbone seventeen feet long. Hector Boethius in his *History of Scotland* claims to have found an entire human skeleton fourteen feet in length. In Lucerne, Switzerland, the physician Plater recorded a human skeleton seventeen feet long. In Bohemia, two human shinbones were found in the eighth century that measured twenty-six feet. That would make that gentleman over one hundred feet tall. A major portion of a human skeleton was found in England in 1171. Erect, he would have stood fifty feet in height. Saint Augustine tells of seeing a human tooth one hundred times normal size on the beach near Utica. Plutarch states that he saw the remains of a human carcass over one hundred feet long. The scientist Kircher reports a human skeleton four hundred feet high found near Palermo, Italy. Near

Damascus, an old priest pointed out to yours truly an ancient grave which the people around there swear is the grave of Abel. I measured it. It was thirty feet long. The supposed grave of Noah was shown to me in Lebanon. By my own measure it was seventy yards in length. The thrust of my research indicates that the stature of men has decreased since man first strode the earth. In 1718, a Frenchman named Henrion stated categorically that Adam and Eve were over one hundred feet tall, Noah and Abraham were over twenty feet, and Moses was thirteen feet tall."

Broderick shook his head in disagreement. "You're talking to a B-plus student in Anthropology I. Nowhere in my texts were giant human forms mentioned. The line from the tree shrew to modern man seemed quite clear."

"Not as clear, Lieutenant, as our arrogance would have us believe. Do you think, my friend, that we have accurately traced every mutated, unsuccessful form of life, human and nonhuman, to its extinction? And when disturbing fossil proofs *do* arise from the rocks, proofs such as I've just recited to you, the frightened world has constantly chosen not to believe."

The lieutenant stared up at Stirner, stroking his moustache moodily. "It's hard, Professor. Very hard. Giant reptiles? Yes. Giant insects? Yes. But . . ."

Stirner's forefinger thrust out toward the seated man. "But that's exactly my *point*, Lieutenant. In prehistoric times almost every form of life, insects, reptiles, plants, mammals, fish, *did* develop a giant form of life. Isn't it conceivable, isn't it probable, that a large form, may I say a giant form, of humanoid life also developed? It was found defective by Nature, like the other giant forms, bigness apparently being not fitness, and became extinct, as did all the others."

"Be specific," Broderick said. "What did they develop from?"

"Specifically, *Australopithecus boisei*."

"What the hell is that?" the lieutenant asked, his head snapping up.

Stirner sighed. "I'll try to keep it short. About five million years ago, our common ancestor, Ramapithecus, a small forest ape, branched out into three separate lines. *Homo habilis,* which developed into Man, *Australopithecus africanus,* and *Australopithecus boisei.* It is this last fellow that interests me. He was a larger specimen than the other two but with a smaller braincase. Three-quarters of a million years ago he was gone. What happened to him before extinction? In those lost, dark eons of time, just how large did he develop? No one is sure. It is my contention that, like the dinosaur, *Australopithecus boisei* may have achieved magnum proportions before he became extinct. He may have achieved a height of ten, twenty, even thirty feet, with a strength that would be indescribable. In fact, a giant. And if this is true, how many of his descendants walk the earth today. Smaller, through intermarriage with humans, but still with that incredible strength." Stirner cleared his throat. "It is my belief that somewhere in the lineage of our night friend out there, there was a giant, an immense being with a strength you cannot possibly conceive, and there is a strong possibility that he possessed a degree of magical powers. That giant's offspring and all subsequent offspring were trolls, some resembling their humanoid parent, some horrible to contemplate. You are aware of the whimsy of the genes. Down through the dusty eons, through multiple thousands of generations, and an equal number of troll-human matings, the giant characteristics have diminished. But the power is still there, the magic is still there, the evil lusts are still there. Ancestral traits die hard or they do not die at all. Our criminal walks like a man, mows his lawn, brushes his teeth, tinkers with his car. But his mind is that of a troll-beast. He cannot escape his heritage. On the contrary, he revels in his heritage."

Christine glanced at the detective. His expression was one of reservation, disbelief. "Is it possible," Broderick wondered, "that you are describing a very disturbed individual, whose dementia gives him an above normal strength?"

"Above normal? To tear the hindquarters off a horse? To annihilate a Great Dane in a matter of seconds? To tear the roof off a car, the head off a dog? Some disturbance. Some dementia. You don't really believe, Lieutenant, that those acts could have been committed by someone like Steinmetz or any other psychopath. Surely you must have been bothered from the very beginning by the sheer physical power you were confronted with?" Almost against his will, Broderick nodded slightly. Seeing this, Stirner continued rapidly. "Do you think for one moment, Lieutenant, that I would be playing detective if I didn't think my intervention was necessary, if I didn't think you were up against something beyond your ken, something beyond 'abnormal'? These deeds reek of the supernatural. They are steeped, as I intend to prove to you, in an aura of mythic legend. Each terrible act fits together like the pieces of some blood-spattered jigsaw puzzle. Even if you were able to put them together, you would not be able to recognize the picture before you. Because of my training, because of specific research I have just completed, I may be able to help you. I have seen that final picture, Lieutenant. My problem is getting you to believe it."

Broderick drummed his fingers on the chair arm, stared out the window. "It's cute," he said finally, "but it doesn't stand up. Giants have never existed on earth. No giants, no offspring. No offspring, no case. It's like telling me that one of the relatives of the seven dwarfs did it. If I reported this to my superiors I'd be patrolling used car lots and junk yards within the hour."

Stirner strode over to his briefcase, removed some papers, and handed them to Broderick. "I told you I was prepared," he said. "That's a condensed version of a one-hundred-page research paper on the probable existence of giants on earth sometime within the last two million years. I ask you to read it. If, when you have finished, you still think I am one of the brothers Grimm, I shall turn in my badge and slink back to my ivy-covered walls. But I am right, Lieutenant. By God, I am right. Read and believe."

17

ore than one hour later, Lieutenant Broderick sat staring at the last page, an unlit cigarette held in his lips. He closed the report delicately, but did not look up. It was several seconds before he looked at Bowen Stirner, who was watching him intently. "If you ever get tired of teaching, Professor," he said, "we can use you down at the DA's office. Giant and Elf Division."

"Do you believe it?" Stirner asked.

The detective lit his cigarette. "I have two questions, Professor. One: Is giant-humanoid copulation anatomically possible, and two: Would the sperm fertilize the ovum to produce a troll offspring?"

Stirner stared down at the seated man. "I am impressed, Lieutenant. You should have been an anthropologist."

Broderick squinted up at him through the smoke from his cigarette. "You find some of us plain folks beyond the walls of academe quite clever, Professor, almost verbal? 'Alleged' and 'perpetrator' are only two out of a hundred words I know. Answer my questions."

Stirner, sensing the seriousness in the other man's voice, answered eagerly. "Fertilization *would* occur. It is highly probable that *habilis* and *boisei* copulated and produced offspring while *boisei* was still at his normal stature."

The detective waved his finger. "Ah, ah, Professor. There is an assumption implied there."

"Agreed. Anatomically, I see no insurmountable problem. What constitutes a giant? We have men today who are seven feet or more. We must assume that they copulate. Then what about an eight-foot man, or even a ten- or fifteen-foot man. With apologies to Mrs. Marino, it might prove uncomfortable, but certainly not impossible. When we get into the fifty- or even the hundred-foot category, we may assume, how shall I say it, difficulties. Either no giant-human copulation occurred at these statures or a human male and a giantess were involved. It would seem unlikely, however."

"As long as someone finally acknowledged my presence, I would like to interject something here from the feminine point." Both men turned toward Christine. "If these beings really did exist, what female human, in her right mind, would—what word are we using today—copulate with them?"

"One does not *choose* one's giant," Stirner said gently. "We can assume forcible rape in most instances. Do not, however, speak to me of right mind when it comes to human sexuality, my dear. If one were to probe the copulative history of the human being through the ages—with its legends of centaurs, minotaurs, harpies, werewolves, mermaids, half the gods of ancient civilizations—one would stagger and retch. Humans have always copulated out of their species. They are doing it now as we speak. We are, Christine, a horny species. The more I researched this, the more I've come to believe our only criteria throughout history has been movement of some sort. Couple this promiscuousness with the unutterably powerful lustings of giants, who are members of the same species, and I have no difficulty imagining their ruttings. The earth must have shaken with them. I am not surprised that trolls exist. I am surprised that there are not more of them."

The detective's eyes remained on Bowen Stirner. "I'd better get out of here," he said finally. "I'm starting to believe you."

Stirner stood up and pointed a finger at the other man. "This is no joke, Lieutenant. What I've told you is factual. Incredible but factual. Believe it. Stop it now. Because if you don't, it will happen again. To a troll, sexual desire is mixed with blood desire. Carnal arousement brings dismemberment, love mingles with twisting and killing and the drinking of blood. Believe it, Lieutenant. Shoot somebody."

Christine's mouth opened, her face was pale as she stared at the two men.

Broderick met the fierce gaze calmly. "Who?" he asked.

There was no hesitation in Stirner's response. "Karl Anderson," he said.

"That's a charge of murder you're making," the detective said evenly. "You must be in possession of facts I am unaware of."

Once again Stirner pointed a finger at the lieutenant. "Anderson is a troll, Broderick. Make no mistake about that. I shall attempt to prove it, but whether I do or not, he's the one. I'm convinced of it."

"Fortunately, Stirner, the days of witch-hunts are over. The police nowadays require proof." He withdrew a small notebook and pen from his jacket pocket.

Stirner's head was nodding impatiently. "All right, all right," he said. "Proof: the physical appearance of the man. The hugeness, that huge, thick neck, the swollen, almost cretinous facial features. Whenever trolls appear in human form, these characteristics match every description I have read about.

"Proof: that horse. Trolls make offerings to their own gods of horror. That horse was hanging in Anderson's boathouse, a desecrated, bloodless offering. That boathouse is some sort of sacrificial site. I can feel the evil there. No wonder crazy Steinmetz loved it so much he cried when you plucked him from it. It was his kind of place.

"Proof: final. Irrevocable. That poem."

"What poem?"

"A poem, Lieutenant, read by a beautiful girl on a sunset beach. That poem is the surest proof of all. Undeniable, metaphysical proof of the terror that lies in my neighbor's heart. The words were spoken by his daughter, but the ideas, the horror, were his. A paean to evil and nihilism and blood. Shoot him, Lieutenant. Solve your case."

Broderick stared at the notes he had taken. "Now let's see if I can piece this together. So far we've got a fat man who's had bad luck with his boathouse and whose daughter writes lousy poems. I wonder if I can make it stick."

Stirner's voice rose in anger. "Now listen, Lieutenant, I don't appreciate your tone. I'm right, damnit. I know it."

Broderick's voice remained calm, but there was a hint of ice in it. "No, you listen, Professor." He flipped the pages of his notebook. "There are a few items I copied from the files of these cases that I'd like you to hear. On the night of March fourth, at six P.M., the approximate time that horse was killed, Mr. and Mrs. Allen Levine attended a dinner party with Mr. and Mrs. George Potts and two other couples at a local restaurant. Seventeen witnesses. They did not arrive home at their respective houses until eleven-twenty P.M. Mr. Maynard Drogin was sick in bed with the flu, no witnesses. Mr. Bowen Stirner was at home correcting papers all evening. No witnesses. Mr. Karl Anderson was in Philadelphia, Pennsylvania, at a jewelers' convention. He spent a total of three days there, March third, fourth, and fifth. There are over thirty witnesses who can place him there on the evening in question.

"On the night of July fifteenth, the night the two young people were killed at twelve-thirty A.M., Mr. George Potts and his wife hosted a party. Among the guests were Mr. Maynard Drogin and Mr. Karl Anderson, who attended from approximately nine o'clock until three o'clock in the morning. Twenty-seven witnesses. Mr. Bowen Stirner was at home correcting papers. No witnesses. You correct a hell of a lot of papers, Professor." The two men's eyes met, Stirner's perplexed, Broderick's steadfast. "On the other two occasions, the killings of the two dogs, Karl Anderson was hosting parties at his home. No constant witness verification. On the whole, Professor, I'd say that you make a much better suspect than Anderson." He paused. "Much better," he stated again.

Stirner's face grew red, his hands clenched into fists. "Are you implying? . . . What are you saying?"

"I am saying, Professor, that from a police point of view, *you* make a hell of a lot better suspect than your friend Anderson."

Seeing the anger mount in Bowen Stirner's face, Christine stared down at the floor. The sudden confrontation between the two men had caught her by surprise, frightened her.

"You must be out of your mind," Stirner exploded. "Would I be here now, trying to help . . ."

"You are here now making accusations, Dr. Stirner. The department does not like accusations that cannot be backed up in court. Now, why don't you calm down? I am not accusing you, Anderson, or anyone else. I am simply doing what I get paid to do. I'm trying to get some facts."

Bowen Stirner sat down, shaking his head. "I don't understand it," he said. "Everything fits. So perfectly. Are you sure those reports are accurate, Lieutenant?"

The detective's moustache twitched once. "What the hell, Professor, do you think we've been doing for the past five months? Sitting on our asses correcting papers? My apologies, Mrs. Marino. You're damn well right they're accurate. Don't you know that everyone in this area has been checked and rechecked many times, including your friend Mr. Anderson? I checked him out myself. He couldn't have killed those kids. It's impossible." Broderick leaned forward. The hardness in his voice was gone. "Let me say this, Dr. Stirner. Nothing in my experience as a law officer has prepared me for the type of crime we are dealing with here. The ferocity. The unnatural power. You haven't seen what I have seen. It is possible that your theory is correct in some measure. You may just have the wrong suspect."

Stirner shook his head again. His fiery confidence was gone. "My theory *has* to be correct, Lieutenant. And I would have bet my life it was Anderson. I don't understand it. I simply do not understand."

The detective stood up and put his notebook back in his pocket. "Professor, I'd like to show your report to my superiors. Something about touching all bases."

Stirner waved his hand distractedly. "Of course."

"Cheer up, Doc. You've given me a few things to think about, a few things to check into. I'll be in touch." He turned toward Christine. "Good-bye, Mrs. Marino. Your company has been, as always, charming. With or without doughnuts."

Christine walked the detective to the door. When she came back to the living room, Bowen Stirner had not moved. She sat in a chair opposite him. "I'm frightened, Bowen. Listening to all this, I'm not sure I can handle it. I want to leave. I'm frightened."

Stirner had not heard her. "It's got to be him, Chris," he said. "It's got to be."

Christine's voice was barely audible. "And if it isn't, Bowen?"

The gray eyes raised slowly to Christine's face. "Then we're back at the beginning. And the beast will roam our lawns. Whoever he is." As traces of fright etched Christine's face, he covered her hands with his. After a long moment, he spoke again. "Did you know, Mrs. Marino, that a great portion of a professor's work is correcting papers? Are you aware of that?"

Christine's eyes widened. "Oh, Bowen, I never . . . Don't even *talk* like that."

Slowly, his hands clenched on hers. "I just thought you should know," he said quietly.

18

From the diary of Henrietta Knapp:

August 21.
Touch of a cold this morning. Small fortification with vodka, hint of cherry cough syrup. Should get it patented. Fell on last stair. Lay quietly—heard everything! Giants? Trolls? My old neighborhood in the Bronx was better than this! Going to check on Anderson myself. Check everybody! Personally, I think it's that Drogin person. Weird individual. Get more cough medicine.

August 22.

What a scene today. Christine wouldn't let Joey go in the car with Nick. Can't blame her. How could one man change so much? Caught in the middle as usual. So upset I forgot to drink anything *today. Catch up tomorrow.*

August 23.

After three days Nick came home. Says he slept in the restaurant. Ha!! *Christine so upset, poor dearie. He looks terrible! What has he been doing!? The way he looks, the way he eats, the way he talks.* Mon Dieu! *He even smells,* que dit on, *a trifle gamey. Passed out on my bed this afternoon (from an experimental drink I shall not even dignify by mentioning) and found the master of the house standing in the doorway positively leering at me!?*

Slight headache. Reading too much?

August 24.

Terrible argument today. Had to take Joey out of the house. The mistress accused him of spending his nights at the Andersons'. Nick now speaks only in obscenities. Situation definitely deteriorating here. I think he's going to harm her. Maybe all of us. Will not desert Christine and Joey. The man is sick! My darling, darling Nick, what has happened?

August 25.

Situation positively gothic. Master gone again, mistress crying. Wind blowing, clouds racing across a

*moon bright as a lunatic's eye, dogs howling somewhere.
I feel like we're in a late-night movie.*

    *Whatever happened to the basics of life? Popcorn,
laughter, Johnny Carson, Christmas carols?*

    Got to get to the bottom of all this!!!

19

The next morning, Christine, Joey, and Henrietta sat at Sunday brunch. Christine was red-eyed and silent. Joey, who had spent the last several days in his room watching television and playing with toys he hadn't touched in years, sat with his head down, picking at his food. From time to time he would lift puzzled eyes toward his mother, but her face did not offer the reassurance he sought. His attention would quickly return to the uneaten food in front of him. Henrietta looked at both of them silently, shaking her head.

The front door opened and slammed shut. There had

been no sound of a car. Christine's mouth tightened.

Nick Marino walked into the kitchen, his suit jacket slung over his shoulder. "Hi, gang," he said. His greeting was met with silence. "Isn't anybody going to say hello to old Nick?"

Joey looked at his father furtively. His eyes widened. He looked down quickly. "Hey, Dad," he said in a barely audible voice. Christine did not look up at her husband.

Henrietta stared at Nick in disbelief. She saw the swollen features, the mouth twisted into a strange smile over the yellow-gleaming teeth. When she saw his eyes, she looked away. It was as if something evil pulsated within him, bulging his face, burning behind his eyes in an effort to burst forth.

"Sport," Nick said, "you're going to spend the afternoon with your father. We'll gather things. And tonight, a barbecue. A veritable feast. I'm going to change my clothes and we'll be on our way." His voice became flat and cold as he turned toward Christine. "Any objections?" Christine still did not look up. Nick left the room and went up the stairs.

Christine and Henrietta sat staring at each other. Then Christine turned to Joey. "Honey, I don't think you ought to go with Daddy today." She tried to keep the fear out of her voice. "Daddy seems a little upset. Maybe some other time."

Joey nodded his head, swallowed, and said nothing. He continued to look down at his plate, his small shoulders hunched forward.

Nick returned to the silent room several minutes later

dressed in blue jeans. He was not wearing shoes or a shirt.

"Ready, Joey?" He grasped the boy by the wrist. Joey looked at his mother in fright.

Christine stood up. "Nick . . ."

Nick's head swiveled toward her. The malignance in his eyes made the words catch in her throat. "What!" His voice was incredibly powerful, a roar. "What, slut?" He stared at her a moment longer and then pulled Joey out the front door as Christine stood transfixed. She heard the car churn pebbles in the driveway.

"Oh my God, Henrietta," Christine said. "I'm going to call the police."

Henrietta's voice was calm. "Take it easy, dearie. What are you going to tell them? That your husband took his son on an outing? I know Nick, honey. He may be upset, but he would never harm Joey. Never."

"Upset!" Christine's voice was shrill. "Damnit, Henrietta, didn't you see him, didn't you hear him? He's crazy. My husband is crazy."

"No," Henrietta said firmly. "He's not crazy. He's as rational as you and I."

"Then what the *hell* would you call it?"

"I don't know," the older woman said quietly. "I wish I did."

Christine spent the afternoon in torment. She sat by the window unmoving for hours. Twice she had the telephone in her hand to call the police and twice she put it down again. At ten minutes after five she heard the car pull into the driveway. Relief flooded through her as she saw Joey in the front seat. A minute later he walked through the front door and started up the stairs.

Christine ran to him and wrapped her arms around him. "Joey," she said. "I'm so glad you're home. Did you have lunch? Do you want something to eat?"

Joey shook his head. He was looking down at his feet.

"Joey, what's wrong? Where did you go?"

Joey shrugged his shoulders. "We went to a farm," he said.

"Oh, that's nice." Christine ruffled the dark hair. "Did you have fun?"

"No," Joey said, quick tears coming to his eyes. Christine sensed that there was something he wanted to tell her but could not. "No, I didn't," he added in a quavering voice. He shook himself free and ran up the stairs.

Christine was close to despair as she watched her tearful son run to his room and slam the door. She knew she had to confront Nick about what had happened, but decided to wait until she had the courage and composure to do it.

Around six o'clock Christine made up her mind to face Nick. She made a platterful of hamburgers and walked to the far end of the patio. Nick was standing several yards from the charcoal fire. He was squatting down, his back to the burning coals. When one of them sputtered and burst into flame, he turned his head toward it quickly, fear and apprehension showing in his face. As she approached him, Christine heard him recite in a low, dull monotone:

> *Take ye out of me stomach and groin,*
> *For go to the Gill will I.*
> *Take you out of me milt and loin,*
> *To Mjoa-firth Gill I hie.*

As Christine stood staring at him, he repeated the verse two more times. My God, she thought, he *is* crazy. How can I talk to him? It was then that she caught the smell of something burning on the grill. The stench was abominable.

Nick turned around slowly, his eyes glinting. "Ah, the lovely bride." He smiled secretly. "Sit down, Christine Marino, and share the fruits of our afternoon's work." He took a long drink from a goblet made from a steer's horn. Christine had never seen it before.

Christine sat down, the platter in her lap. "Nick, I made some hamburgers. What are you cooking? It smells awful."

"Matter of opinion, slut woman. Matter of opinion." Using a long, sharpened branch, he speared one of the round, flat things on the grill. Christine noticed the consternation on his face as the fire sparked briefly. He snatched the object off the end of the stick and juggled it like a hot piece of toast. Then he took a large bite from it. "Not bad," he said. "Really not bad for cow shit."

Christine stared at him in horror, her hand covering her mouth.

"Have I offended thee, slut? Then be doubly offended." He walked over to her and pushed her head toward the goblet in his hand. The smell was unmistakable. "Horse piss," he said. "Sharp, pungent. Clears the head."

Christine retched, tried to get up. Nick yanked her back into her seat by her hair.

"Leaving before the main course? What an impolite whore you are." Nick shook his head. "Shows very poor breeding. You would never make it in the restaurant business. As I have." He released her roughly and walked over to a bag lying at the base of the grill. He reached in and withdrew several large dead toads. Christine watched in utter loathing as he tossed them onto the grill. Unable to move, she watched them burn and burst, hissing the bright red coals beneath them. Her mouth opened in a silent scream. Finally she managed to stand up, the platter shattering on the bricks below, and run toward the house.

Nick Marino did not see her go. He raised the horn in a silent toast toward the sky, and then poured its contents over his face and mouth, lapping at the cascading liquid eagerly.

20

*M*ethodically, almost numbly, Christine unpacked the last of the valises and stored them back in the closet. She sat down on the bed, too tired to move. Her mind dimly recalled the events of the past twelve hours: Nick's obscene behavior, her hurried, hysterical packing, the apology and agreement to see a psychiatrist right away. "We'll call tomorrow for an appointment immediately after this Labor Day weekend," he had promised. "Apparently I need more help than I thought," he had said.

Christine had spent a sleepless night wondering

whether to believe Nick or leave him. But that morning Nick had stood beside her as she made an appointment with Kimberly Potts's psychiatrist, Dr. Ernst Nieuman, for the following Tuesday morning.

"Are you sure you want to do this?" Christine had asked. "Will you go?"

"Of course I will," was his reply. "His diagnosis should prove interesting."

She looked at the disarrayed clothes that had been tossed on the bed. Where would I have gone anyway, she wondered sadly. She sat up and squared her shoulders. Things could not possibly get worse, Christine thought wryly, so they have to get better.

At least money was no problem. Loreto Marino was sending Nick's salary to Christine each week, until he "straightened out with the shrink." When Christine had called to thank him, he had threatened to hang up if she mentioned it again.

Joey was out of Nick's sight much of the time. He had joined a soccer league and spent several hours every day practicing with boys his own age, away from the House of Horrors.

Still, Christine found it difficult to relax. She took out her paints, setting her easel in the sunlit part of the terrace, eyeing the picture in front of her from beneath her baseball cap. On Labor Day, two days from now, the annual Mill Harbor Charity Art Show was going to be held in the town park, and Christine had been asked to exhibit her work. She had shyly tried to decline but Kimberly Potts had been insistent.

"It will cheer you up, girl," she had told Christine over the telephone. "You've been looking a little down lately. Besides, I've seen your work. You're good." Christine had finally accepted. Secretly she was proud to have been asked.

Saturday morning dawned hot and humid, threatening rain. Large, dark clouds loomed motionless over the Sound, but here and there long shafts of sunlight silvered the water. One of those on my paintings would help, Christine thought as Joey and Henrietta helped her load them carefully into the station wagon.

Kimberly and George Potts were the first people she knew to walk past her display. Kimberly took Christine aside while her husband scrutinized the paintings carefully.

"Did you hear?" Kimberly said. "The Brewers and the Melnicks have put their houses up for sale. After what happened to the teenagers. You're staying, aren't you, Chris?"

"I don't know," Christine said, looking down. "My life is somewhat of a mess right now, Kim, and I didn't have much courage to start with."

"Nick?" the other woman asked.

"Yes. Without him I'm afraid I'm not very sturdy."

"Bullshit," Kimberly Potts said firmly. "I know you. You'll stay, with or without Nick."

"How about you and George?"

"Are you kidding? George says he's got too much invested here to be chased out by some nut."

Christine looked at the dapper little man. "I think,

Mrs. Potts, that your husband is tougher than he looks."

George Potts called out to her. "Christine. How much is that one over there? The one with the little boy leaving footprints on that lonely beach. I like it."

"Sixty-five dollars," Christine said timidly.

"What? I didn't hear you."

"One hundred dollars," Kimberly Potts shouted. "Buy it, George. I love it."

"A hundred? I can't buy anything at list price. It hurts me physically. I'll give you a check for eighty-five dollars right now. Take it or leave it."

"You're tougher than you look, George," Kimberly said, winking at Christine. "Make it out to the Mill Harbor Charity Fund."

After they had left, Christine felt a small surge of pride. Damnit, she thought, I don't care if they were just trying to be nice. I sold one. I actually sold one.

To Christine's amazement she had sold three more paintings by the time she saw Bowen Stirner's bronzed head coming toward her above the crowd. To her surprise, he was walking unsteadily.

"Why, Doctor," she said, as his kiss lingered on her cheek, "how charming for your liver to be plastered by one o'clock. I think you're turning into a loser."

"No loser I, Chris, love. Mad I, confused I, very angry I, but a winner in the hearts of my countrymen, who love me. Are you a countryman—country person?"

"I'm a successful person. I've sold four paintings, Bowen."

"That's nice." Stirner had barely heard her. He was looking intently through the crowds of people at the various booths.

Christine looked at him closely. "What's the matter, Bowen?" she asked quietly.

"Gall." His eyes returned to hers. "For the last few days I've been breathing and eating gall. I think I was drinking it this morning. That son of a bitch is getting away with murder, Chris."

"What are you talking about? Who?"

"Anderson!" he exploded. "Anderson kills and gets away with it. And the bastard will do it again, Chris, unless we stop him."

"Who will?"

Stirner wheeled around toward the voice behind him.

Lieutenant Broderick was standing behind him looking down at one of Christine's paintings speculatively. "Who will?" he repeated.

"You know damn well who I'm talking about, Lieutenant."

"Look, Dr. Stirner, I've warned you before. Now I'm making it official. No more charges unless you can back them up with proof. Proof that will stand up in court. You understand?"

"I guess the official way is to wait patiently to be murdered in our beds. I understand."

The detective's face hardened. He looked at the swaying man in front of him carefully for a moment and then said softly, "I turned in your report, Dr. Stirner."

"And?"

"Officially, it's under advisement. Unofficially . . . well . . ."

"They don't believe it."

"I'm afraid giants and trolls are not the in thing with the Nassau County Police Department this year."

"You see, Chris?" Stirner said loudly. "He's going to get away with it. It's just a question of who's next."

"Easy, Doc, easy," the detective said. "You might be interested to know that I've been doing a little investigating on my own time. Public servant, you understand. I find it, unofficially now, just a little interesting that Karl Anderson has moved three times in the past seven years."

Stirner turned and faced the lieutenant, his eyes alert, eager.

"I find it interesting, Doctor," the detective continued, "that before each move, once in Ohio, once in Vermont, there seems to have been a record of incidents involving pets and larger animals. In Vermont, a neighbor's small child disappeared. It could be coincidence, of course, but I assure you, I am going to continue my investigations. I need more time."

Stirner shook his head vehemently. "We don't have time, Lieutenant. Shoot the bastard, kill the beast. Then pursue your investigations."

Broderick looked at Christine. "Public intoxication is never a pretty sight, is it? Mrs. Marino, why do most of your paintings have footprints in them?"

Christine, who had been listening intently, blinked

several times. "What? Oh. It's symbolism. After listening to you two, the meaning escapes me for the moment."

"I like the one on the end. The sunset. How much is it?"

"Twenty-five dollars," she murmured.

"I'm sorry, I didn't hear you. How much?"

Christine cleared her throat. "Twenty-five dollars."

"Sold." The detective drew out his wallet.

"Lieutenant," Christine said, "you don't have to . . ."

"I know, Mrs. Marino. The fact is, I want to."

Christine watched the detective as he walked toward his car with her painting. You've got to stop being amazed when people buy your paintings, old girl, she thought. The fact is, you're a pretty decent painter. She turned to Stirner. "Bowen," she said, "he just bought . . ." Christine stopped. The look on Bowen Stirner's face was deadly. She followed his gaze into the crowd and saw Karl Anderson walking toward them. On his arm, cool and beautiful as ever, was his daughter. Anderson's bulk was covered by a black sports jacket and yellow slacks. The silver hair lay close to the huge skull. The crystal eyes gleamed above the high cheekbones.

"Mrs. Marino," he said. "And the eminent Dr. Stirner. What a handsome couple you make. Dazzling, in fact. You do not answer. Ah. Cat's got your tongue? Lucky cat. And where is your husband, my dear Christine? The eminent Nick. He missed his guitar lesson today." He turned to the girl at his side. "I think today they were going to harmonize together."

Not a flicker on either one of their faces, Christine noted. How stoic of them. "He's not here," she said. "He went to work today." She faced the girl. "The first time in days. He's been upset lately. Some disease, no doubt." The girl's face remained expressionless.

Anderson smiled. "I see that you paint, Mrs. Marino. I've watched you often enough on the beach. I'd like to buy one. That painting of the lighthouse intrigues me."

"They're not for sale." Stirner's voice was loud, abrasive.

Anderson turned slowly and faced Stirner. His features were impassive, his voice controlled. "What did you say?"

"I said, they're not for sale. I've bought them all. I just decided."

The smile returned to Anderson's face with difficulty. "How gallant of you. How wealthy of you. I hear that you're somewhat of an artist yourself, Stirner." His eyes regarded the other man closely. "When you're sober, I hear that you write. I hear that you're a writer of fiction. Fairy tales about giants, dwarfs. Fee, fie, fo, fum, and all that."

"What!" Stirner shouted angrily. "Where did you get your hands on that? That report was turned into the police."

"Let's just say that I have friends in high places."

Stirner's face flushed. Fear and anger played about his features. Christine pressed his hand to keep him from speaking.

"Well, this has been a nice little chat," said Karl Anderson. "It's always fun when neighbors get together. Mrs. Marino, as always, the sight of you has enchanted my day." He grasped his daughter firmly by the arm. As they walked away, her head remained turned toward Stirner, her eyes lingering on him malevolently. Christine had never seen such a strange, chilling look. A wild but muted hatred that transformed the perfect features into imperfection.

Bowen Stirner saw it too. "My God, did you see her face, Christine?"

"I saw it," Christine replied. It had sent fear down to the depths of her being.

It was five o'clock when the first few drops of rain came. Dark clouds were racing across the sky from Connecticut, threatening a heavy rain. Thunder rumbled toward them across the Sound.

Christine, Henrietta, and Joey ran feverishly back and forth to and from the car, carrying the remaining paintings. As Christine was about to go back for the last one, she saw Bowen Stirner carrying it toward her.

"Chris," he said, "can you give me a ride home? The people I came with seem to have disappeared."

"Of course," Christine said. She leaned over and unlocked the door. In the general rush and excitement, Christine pumped the gas pedal several times. When she turned the key, the car coughed but would not start.

"You've flooded the engine, my dear," Bowen Stirner said with a smile.

"I know what I've done, Professor Stirner," she answered. "Flooding this engine seems to be a habit of mine. I only do it when I'm nervous."

"Interesting," Stirner said musingly.

After waiting two minutes, Christine tried to start the car again. The motor roared into life and she pulled away from the curb.

The rain began slowly. As she drove over the wet road, Christine could feel Bowen Stirner's eyes on her. Finally, he spoke.

"If it's all right with you-know-who in the back seat, Mrs. Marino, I'd like you to come over to my house after you drop Joey and you-know-who off. It will only take half an hour or so."

"I'll bet." A crisp voice came from the back seat.

Christine looked into the rearview mirror. "Henrietta!" she said.

"Will you tell that lovely but suspicious woman that I have something I want you to read. That it concerns your husband, Nick. Yes, I know he's in trouble. I've seen him. I've watched him. I think I may be able to help him."

"If this is a line," Henrietta said, "it's disgusting."

"No line, Auntie. Strictly on the level."

"I give up," Henrietta said. "But I'm still going to time you."

Christine drove straight into the garage. They unloaded the pictures and Henrietta promised to start the dinner.

Stirner looked up at the dark sky. "The rain's stopped for a while. C'mon, Chris, you've been sitting all day. Let's walk over." When Christine nodded, he cupped his hands to his mouth. "Did you hear that, timekeeper? We're walking. I need another twenty minutes."

"You got fourteen," the equally loud answer came from inside the kitchen.

The path that led along the shore was shrouded in mist. The air was humid and smelled of cedar, pines, and the sea. The blackening sky was filled with glory: blue sunlit patches, shining, disappearing, soft-hued layers of clouds shifting about each other in gigantic caress. Sudden flashes of lightning illumined the towering cloudbanks for brief moments.

"Oh, Bowen, look," Christine said, pointing to a rainbow that arched toward the earth.

"Beautiful," he said. His arm went around her waist in a natural gesture, and they continued to walk, looking up at the sky.

After several minutes of silence, Christine said, "Bowen, what is it you want me to read?"

"We'll discuss it after you've read it. Nick's in trouble. Deep trouble. And I don't know how to get him out of it. Not yet. But I can tell you this. He's not crazy. And whatever he's done, well, it's not his fault. He's not to be blamed for his actions."

"I don't understand," Christine said.

"You will," he answered.

As the path took them past the Anderson boathouse, Christine shivered. "After what happened to that horse, this place terrifies me. I heard you mention it to Lieutenant Broderick. What did you call it?"

Stirner stopped and stared at the rain-dripping, flaking building. "A sacrificial site? Perhaps. Want to go in and check it out?"

"Are you kidding?" Christine said, looking up at him. She had never seen his face more determined, his eyes more serious. It had started to rain again, gently.

"If I had any guts, I'd go in there right now. If you weren't here . . ."

A vivid flash of lightning lit up the boathouse at that moment. They stared at the gaping-mouth doorway, the boarded windows, the wooden heads that encircled the eaves. The loud rumble of thunder that followed startled Christine. Stirner's arm around her waist tightened in reassurance, then gradually turned her around to face him. Christine raised her head. The rain formed small rivulets on her face, blinking her eyes. Stirner leaned down and kissed her. It was a long, sexual kiss. She did not resist. She participated. Another flash of lightning bathed the beach in light, silhouetting their clinging bodies in a white glare in front of the dark boathouse entrance.

And then it was over. They continued to walk, Christine looking at the ground in front of her, Stirner with his lips pressed to her hair.

When they reached his house, Christine stopped. "Bowen, I . . ." She paused.

"I know, I know." Stirner tried unsuccessfully to smile. "It was a mistake. We got carried away. You're married. You love your husband and your son. Blame the lightning, fault the thunder. Is that what you were going to say?"

"Something like that, yes."

"Have no fear, beautiful Christine. My heart has been a stick of wood since Livia Fletcher broke it in the sixth grade. I have felt nothing since." He opened the front door. "To allay your fears, I shall not go in with you. There is something I have to do. What I want you to read is on the desk in the library. First room on your right."

"Where are you going?" Christine asked.

"Read it," he said. "I'll be back when you're finished. *Ciao*, my pretty." He turned on the hall light and closed the door quietly.

Stirner retraced his footsteps along the path. He paid no attention to the fog, the soft rain. Damn, he thought. Never play around with a beautiful woman. He remembered the wet, upturned face, the cool, perfect mouth, the feel of her body in his arms. He felt exhilarated. Had love finally found Bowen Stirner? He smiled. "Damn fool," he said out loud. "Crazy, damn fool." He lifted his face to the warm drops, to the thunder that rolled down to him from the sky.

When he reached the boathouse he stopped. I should go in there, he thought. That is what I came for. He did not move. The structure had an ominous, physical presence, a terror hidden within its black recesses that emanated outward into the mist. Tomorrow, Stirner decided. I couldn't see anything in there tonight, anyway.

As he turned to go, a voice, feral, primeval, issued from the cavernous entrance.

"Hello, lover," it said.

Stirner wheeled around, startled. The boathouse gleamed in the lightning-rippled air. "Who's there?" he said. He received no answer. "Who the hell is in there?" he repeated. There was only silence. Stirner stood rigid, his face pale. "What do you want?" he said finally, his voice unsteady.

A deep, menacing rumble came from the darkness within. At the sound, a look of recognition flashed across Stirner's eyes. Stark, unreasoning fear distorted his features. "No!" he exhaled into the night. It was a plea, a cry of terror sent up to the dark, shifting sky. He turned and ran along the fog-shrouded path.

The rain was coming down harder now. Thick clouds roiled overhead, groaning with thunder. When he had gone two hundred yards, breathless, he stopped at the top of a small knoll. Looking back through the rain, he saw no sign of anything following him. He was about to continue when he noticed the tops of the rushes near the boathouse wave and thrash. As he watched, unable to move, he saw that something was coming toward him through the rushes. Branches crackled, the tall reeds trembled and disappeared. Stirner's face betrayed his fear. The thing that hurtled toward him was traveling at a speed he could not believe.

Stirner began to run again. His eyes were wide, his face contorted, his mouth gasping for breath. He knew it was useless. He could not escape. Behind him a gutteral bellow rent the air. He stopped, petrified, and turned. A long, pulsating flash of lightning whitened the beach as a figure, its face an illumined savagery, burst from the rushes, all the hell-horrors of earth in one lunging, glistening form.

Stirner raised his hand to ward off the oncoming apparition. His outstretched hand was seized in a grip that squirted the blood from the tips of his fingers. A hand reached for his agonized face. A finger went into his mouth, another entered the socket of his right eye.

The thunder that followed the lightning was directly overhead, the sudden noise shivering the water, shaking the earth.

The decapitated head of Bowen Stirner did not hear it.

21

Christine entered the library and switched the desk lamp on. The report lay on the glass top, glaring in the bright light. She looked at it. I don't want to read it, she thought. I'm frightened enough without any more theories, any more ghouls. She glanced, almost shyly, about the room. The definite bachelor abode. Uncountable pipes, spilled tobacco, coffee cups in odd places, the inevitable mounted trout. Planning to redo, Christine? She shook her head and smiled wryly. A kiss among civilized people, an invitation to the dance, but don't start redecorating, kid. She nodded her head in agreement with herself, sat down at the desk, and opened the report. A note was attached to the first page.

To: Lt. Broderick,
"The capability of believing the unbelievable is the attribute of the intelligent mind."

Bowen Stirner

"Shoot to kill."

Bowen Stirner

Trolls have inhabited the earth since Time's antiquity. Although most major cultures have recorded them in their written history in one form or another, the word "troll" comes to us from the ancient Nordic myths in which these creatures played a large part in the folklore and religions of the people of the northern countries of Europe.

The northmen described trolls in many ways: hulking, evil creatures living in icy mountain caves, or gigantic, magical beast-men living in frozen palaces at the edge of the world. These legends are myriad and conflicting. In an attempt to create order from this disorder, my research indicates the following: Just as Man is the middle ground between dwarf and giant, and combines the characteristics of the two, trolls are the middle ground between Man and giant.

Physically, they are the result of giant-hominoid intercourse. They resemble their progenitors, having a human form and a giant's strength. Their size and strength have been greatly diluted by uncountable generations of troll-hominoid intercourse and further so by troll-hominoid–hominoid intercourse. There are many recorded examples which would indicate that the chromosomes do not always divide so complacently. The results have been monsters staggering to the imagination. I shall not dwell on them here because they do not appear to be part of the current problem.

Mentally, the giant-hominoid amalgam has worked to the detriment of the offspring. The mind of Man, with its superior intellect, its capacity for horror and glory, coupled with the brooding, insolent, dreamy, overbearing, dull-witted untamedness of the giant, has produced a third entity, which combines the worst qualities of its forebears into a personality that would astound either of them.

Trolls are evil, brutal beings, hostile to Man. They have a taste for blood and will kill men and animals to quench this thirst. They have a particular antagonism toward children and will attack them without provocation. They regularly practice human and animal sacrifice, tearing the heads off and placing them on stakes, or hanging the mutilated bodies by their feet as offerings to their gods. Horses tend to be their favorite subject for sacrifice.

Trolls have an abhorrence for the name of Jesus and the sound of church bells. Their greatest fear is that of fire, stemming, possibly, from their earliest beginning when sunlight would destroy them.

Trolls have the unbridled sexual lusts of their giant ancestors. Usually, the object of their desires is taken by direct attack. Killing and the drinking of the victim's blood often accompany these rapes. The humans they lust after are not always killed, however. There is evidence that they are capable of forming strong attachments to certain individuals. When this occurs, attempts are made to transform these individuals into trolls themselves. This transference is accomplished in the following manner: Pulling on the subject's arms and legs, while rubbing him with secret unguents, and howling in his ear. This may continue for hours at a time.

Christine stopped reading. She listened to the rain beating at the windows as it mixed with the soft, continuous thunder overhead. In the recesses of her mind, ideas, remembrances called gently to her, tolling like a steady, distant bell in some hidden mountain valley. Transference? Howling? How many nights had she lain awake on her bed listening to that low howling, waiting for Nick to come home. Nick! What had Bowen Stirner said? *I have something I want you to read. It concerns your husband, Nick.* Drawn like magnets, her eyes returned to the report.

The transformation from human to troll-human is gradual, requiring two full lunar cycles. Physically, the subject will experience a coarsening of facial features, a thickening of the neck and hands. The great strength of the troll is not generally deemed to be transferable.

The behavioral characteristics of the subject will deteriorate at a steadily increasing rate as he assumes the characteristics of his mentors. Both in action and in language the neophyte troll will betray the chaos created within his being as new value systems replace old ones and new and terrifying yearnings form in the depths of his soul.

Christine closed her eyes. The bells were above her now. Their clangor was inescapable, unbearable. Nick! Nick! The incredible, unbelievable bastards have got my Nick! He's not crazy. No nervous breakdown. It's them. The evil Andersons. They've got my Nick.

As she continued to read, her face was drawn in fear and hate.

Unlike either of their human or giant forebears, trolls have developed a high degree of magical powers. They can assume a facial mask, called a grima, or trollsham, and appear as other individuals or as animals. Female trolls are particularly adept at magic. They are reported to ride through the night on the backs of wolves, using snakes as bridles and wearing the grima of a fox or a pig. Being as lustful after humans as the male, they have developed the ability to transform their entire bodies from their horrible actuality into a form that would attract the male human. Additionally, they have developed a magical power to bewitch their sexual prey by singing, which places the object of their desires in total thrall. The legendary sirens of the Rhine and those encountered by Ulysses, who drained and ate their prey, would be examples of troll women in a state of transformation.

Once again Christine stopped reading. She saw a warm, summer afternoon, a beach. Karla Anderson's wordless, beautiful song lilting across the sand. The silent, frozen people. The slow, reluctant raising of Nick's eyes. And before that, Nick's head resting on her thigh as they sat by the swimming pool. The clouded eyes, the masked, troubled face. Once more those beautiful notes. Thrall. Enchantment. Oh, my God, she thought. Bowen, you're right. She's done this to him. He never left us. She took him by magic. Nick never had a chance.

She looked down again at the report.

Conclusion: Trolls exist in the world today. Whether they came from the frigid lands of the North or arose from robust giant ancestors on the plains of Africa is of little consequence. They are among us. And wherever they enter the society of Man, their very nature dictates that malignant murder must follow. And they murder again and again and again. They are not caught, they are not prosecuted. How could they be? No one believes that they exist.

Christine closed the report. She looked out the window. They are among us. She felt cold. They are among us. I'm frightened, she thought. I've never been so frightened. The rain seemed to claw at her as it pounded on the glass, the lightning illumined a dozen grinning, murderous faces pressed to the panes. Where was Bowen? He should have returned by now. She stood up. The fear was a physical pain now that racked her body. She could not stay alone in the house a moment longer. She would phone Bowen in the morning. I've got to get home. Her lips formed the words.

Christine walked briskly, then ran along the path in the pelting rain. She slipped several times, hurting her knee on the sharp shell fragments. At her side, the wind whipped the tops of the tall rushes in frenzied patterns. The thunder was more distant now, occasional flashes of lightning silhouetting huge masses of clouds on the horizon. When she came to the boathouse, she stopped for breath. She was surprised to hear that she was sobbing. She clenched her fists and closed her eyes. Control. No hysteria, she told herself. And then she felt it. There was somebody there with her, standing somewhere in the shadowed night. Silent, watching. She heard her name called, twice, in a voice that came from the interiors of dark caves, the depths of nightmare. Blind terror jolted through her. She began to run again, hearing nothing, seeing nothing. She ran past the boathouse, through the corral, and up the driveway to her home. She pounded on the door, crying, almost sinking to her knees, afraid to look back into the darkness.

One hand resting on a branch above his head, the figure of a man stood at the edge of the wood watching the woman in the doorway. His face, body, and trousers were drenched with blood that the rain could not wash off. His eyes glowed redly in the tidal-scented fog. On his face was the sad, lost look of a lovestruck schoolboy.

22

Christine was awakened the next morning by the sun streaming across her eyes and the loud, insistent singing of birds. The events of the previous day pressed into her sleep-misted brain. Sunshine? she thought. Birds singing? The air from the open window smelled washed clean. To hell with the beasts, she thought. Fight the beasts. She walked sleepily to her bureau and stared at herself in the mirror. With what, old girl? How do you fight sorcery, beast-magic? Think of something. It's now or never.

She went downstairs and started a huge breakfast. Nick and Joey's favorite: cheese omelettes, toasted bagels, fresh coffee. When everything was prepared, she went upstairs, awakened Joey with a kiss, received the accustomed groan, and tiptoed into the guest room.

Christine stared down at her sleeping husband. Nick. You never stopped loving me, she thought. You were attacked, my darling. The insidious night serpents crept into your ear with their night music, their damned witchcraft. She shook her head and bit her lip against the sadness that welled up within her suddenly. This was no nightmare. This was real. She stared at the bulbous features in the once handsome face, the unkempt hair, the thickened neck. She bent down and kissed his forehead. Nick's eyes shot open immediately, his head reared back. My God, Christine thought, he's going to hiss.

"What is it?" Nick demanded warily.

"It's breakfast, Nick," Christine said, managing a smile. "Come and eat breakfast with Joey and me." As she walked out of the room, her smile faltered. His eyes and head had followed her like a snake about to strike.

Despite Christine's efforts at cheerful small talk, breakfast was a miserable affair. Nick was brooding, silent. Joey stole fearful, puzzled glances at his father's face. Christine tried. The starting of school tomorrow, the summer soccer league finals that afternoon. Love, family, and the home, she thought. That's all I know. Can love conquer evil magic? She looked at Nick's face. Love is losing.

When Nick went upstairs to dress, Christine thought of Bowen Stirner. Bowen would know what to do.

Some incantation, perhaps. Some hex sign. Maybe a magic circle. She'd accept any idea, try anything at this point. She telephoned his home. No answer. Where are you, Bowen, when I need you? Her hand still on the telephone, Christine sat and thought. Back to the basics. She knew she could get through to Nick, if she could only be with him alone, talk to him. They had loved each other too much. There must be something left of this deep inside of him. She made up her mind.

Much to Christine's surprise, Nick accepted her suggestion that they take a walk together. As they moved across the lawn toward the corral, Christine talked. Nick said nothing. She talked about the house, the lawn, Joey, plans for the future. It was no good. It was like being with someone she had never known, some sly and ominous stranger. Christine steeled herself. No matter what Nick said or did, she would get through to him. She had to.

When they reached the corral, Christine turned toward Nick and put a hand on his arm. "Kiss me, Nick," she said quietly. "It's been such a long time."

Nick's head swung toward her angrily. "You haven't been exactly keen for my favors during the last few weeks, wife of mine."

"Then do me just a small favor, husband of mine. Kiss me. Now."

Nick inclined his head forward. Christine saw the cruel, heavy-lidded eyes, the swollen features above her. She blinked once, then closed her eyes. They kissed. Nick held her head in callous bondage. Christine was shocked but silent under the alien mouth.

When he finally released her, they stood staring into each other's eyes. Christine's heart leaped. She had seen something, a glimmer of an emotion. Something.

"Christine." The sound of his voice brought Christine's hand to her mouth. It was Nick. But a small, frail voice, a little boy, lost in a trackless fog.

"Kiss me again, Nick," Christine said. She thrust herself forward, caring about nothing but finding the owner of that lost voice.

When they parted once more, Christine's eyes searched Nick's face. Again she saw that soft glow deep within his eyes. Nick raised his hands and caressed the sides of her face, slowly, deliberately. There was a rapt expression on his features, like a child remembering something. But even as she watched, the expression disappeared. A malignant shadow fell over his face, veiling his eyes. Christine felt a terrifying chill as she watched the dark magic recapture his being. His hands continued their downward motion until his fingertips rested on her neck. They paused there, pressing lightly. She saw his eyelids flutter, his lips part in muted rapture. Oh, my God, she thought. He's feeling my pulse. I have lost him to the blood beasts. She controlled her impulse to scream and run. Instead, she gripped his hands gently in her own.

"Nick," she said, looking into that rapt face. "I know what's happened. I know everything. I know about Karl Anderson and his daughter. I know what they've done to you."

If he was surprised, Nick did not show it. His hands fell from her neck and gripped the corral railing. His eyes, in that swollen face, shone brightly. "And what has happened to old Nick?" he asked.

"They've . . . changed you, Nick. They've made you one of them. I'm not sure how. Bowen can explain it to you."

"Ah, Bowen." He did not look at her.

Christine, wanting to touch him, did not. "You don't belong with them, Nick. You belong with Joey and me. You love me, Nick. Come back to me."

Nick's head turned toward her slowly. His eyes were mocking. "Love," he said. "Poor, pallid woman. 'I love you, Nick. I love you, too, Christine. Please pass the salt. Is today really Tuesday?'" His face passed into darker shadows. "Do you have any conception, Christine, of the passion I felt just now as I felt the blood coursing through your delicious arteries? Can you even conceive of the boundless depths of desire that have been opened to me?"

Christine shook her head, her eyes wide with fear and despair. "Blood," she said. "Love and blood and passion. It's evil, Nick. It's demonic."

Nick threw his head back. "Ha! Demonic! Yes, yes. The passion of the daemon. A passion for blood, a passion for rampage, a passion for the night. That is my love, Christine."

"You love God, Nick. You believe in God."

His head swept around in stiff, reptilian fashion, his eyes cold. "I believe in trunt, trunt, and the trolls in the fels."

Despite her sudden fear, Christine heard the recitative quality in his voice. He's been rehearsed, she thought. "You believe in God, Nick. You always have and you always will."

"The trolls in the fels are my gods, you slut," he shouted. He slapped her viciously across the face. Christine's knees sagged, tears came to her eyes. For the first time, she felt the reality of her loss, her utter helplessness.

Nick watched her with cruel intensity. "Ah, the slut understands. Finally. I shall phrase it jubilantly. We are . . . no longer a pair. My heart belongs to someone else. And your heart, tearful whore, belongs to someone else. Yes. You are not forgotten."

"What . . . what do you mean?"

"Ah. That is my secret. Answerable tomorrow upon my graduation. You shall be a small gift from me, a token of my appreciation."

Christine looked at him, bewildered. "'Graduation'? What are you talking about?"

"I am talking about secrets, you prying slut. Secrets that would tremble the lips of your vagina, no longer mine. Black secrets, frost secrets, slime secrets, star secrets, secrets of the bowel, the worm, the firmament." His eyes had a wild, glazed look. "There are secrets all around us, Christine. Everywhere the sweet lips whisper. I can put my ear to the earth and hear the dead as they whimper and complain. Do you know there is a giant hag who sits on the harbor lighthouse on moonless nights. She can drown a child by pointing her finger. I have swum out to her and suckled at her teats. And when the night wind flutters the willow leaves, I can hear their thousand high voices. They are querulous, vicious, but they know the future."

"No, Nick. This is crazy. They've tricked you, hypnotized you, bewitched you with magic . . ." Christine stopped. Nick had turned toward her again, the smile on his face causing the words to catch in her throat. Fresh fear invaded her like flowing electricity.

"Hypnotized? Bewitched? Infantile slut, your naiveté is offensive." He raised his voice in a gutteral shout. "Are there fairies in the bottom of your garden, whore?" That terrible smile. "You did mention magic, didn't you? Want to see a card trick? A multicolored handkerchief, perhaps? No? You are a silent whore, aren't you. Hmmm. Say, here's a dandy." He closed his eyes for several moments, then took several long deep breaths. With each breath his head swelled, perceptibly, until it appeared to be twice its normal size, his features distorted, his eyes like glittering pinpoints. Christine watched in horrified fascination, unable to move. With a long exhalation of fetid air, Nick's head returned to its normal size, the mad smile still on his face. Christine wanted to run but her legs would not move.

"If you liked that one, you'll love this. Look at me, slut." With one hand he grasped Christine's chin and raised it toward his eager, maniacal face. She saw his lips part. Slowly, tentatively, his tongue came out, black, unbelievably long. It explored his face like a restless snake, probing his eyes and nose, leaving a trail of spittle in its wake. Nick's eyes closed as if he were receiving a sexual caress. He unzipped his pants. Christine cried out in terror as his sexual organ, like another long, black snake, raced out of the open fly and wrapped itself twice around his thigh, constricting it tightly. Christine closed her eyes, trying to keep from fainting. She heard Nick's voice. "Want to fool around, slut?" There was a grunting laugh. "Open your eyes, bitch. That's just trickery, illusion, cheap sorcery. I'm still learning. I said, open your eyes."

Christine had one arm around the corral railing. She kept her eyes tightly closed. "Oh, my God, Nick," she said. In the silence that followed she had a premonition that Nick would strike her again. She opened her eyes to find him looking at her thoughtfully, his zipper closed, his tongue returned to his mouth.

"I can do another thing which will amuse the slut," Nick said, as a slow, malicious grin spread across his face. "Don't move. You'll spoil the fun."

Christine watched him walk to the far end of the corral. She felt physically powerless, her legs could barely support her. She watched in silent anguish as Nick sat down on the ground, raised his feet above and behind his head, and then lifted himself off the ground using his hands. It was grotesque. When he started walking around on his hands, uttering duck noises, pig noises, it became obscene. Christine watched him in horror and disbelief.

After almost a minute of this, Nick turned and faced Christine. The noises in his throat grew in volume until he was bellowing like a bull. Then he started toward her slowly at first, then, incredibly, faster and faster.

Christine stared in open-mouthed terror at the horrendous figure hurtling toward her, the wild eyes, the foot-hands. She heard the hellish roar issuing from the open mouth. Her head echoed with the silent scream that could not pass her lips. With a supreme effort she leaped through the railings of the corral. Behind her she heard Nick crash into the wood where she had just been standing. Her mouth open, her eyes wide, she raced toward the house in a panic. Hearing nothing behind her, Christine glanced back over her shoulder. Nick was still in the corral, in that impossible posture, a broken railing in front of him. He was bleeding from the forehead as he stared after her.

Christine slammed the front door behind her and ran into the kitchen. She looked around helplessly, glancing at everything, at nothing. The tears came; she could not stop them. They were tears of fright and sadness. That hellish thing out there had been Nick. Her fist went to her mouth to silence her deepening sobs. Always in the past, for life's big and little terrors, there had been Nick. And now?

Bowen! She ran to the phone, dialed the wrong number twice, steadied her hands, and finally heard his phone ringing. It continued to ring. Where the *hell* was Bowen? She disconnected and dialed the police station, asking for Lieutenant Broderick. Christine shook her head in panic. Lieutenant Broderick was off today, could someone else help? She thanked the officer and hung up. Who else would believe her? They'd think she was crazy.

As Christine's mind slowly stopped racing, one

thought emerged clearly. Get out! Run! Take Joey and Henrietta and run. Away from the trolls, away from Nick, away from terror.

She ran up the stairs to Joey's room. He was sitting on the edge of his bed in his soccer uniform, putting on his sneakers.

"Hi, Mom," he said. "I got a game this morning. Can you take me over to the field?"

Christine shook her head for too long a time. "No," she said finally. "Not today. We're going to visit Aunt Jody for a few days. I want you to come down with me now and get in the car."

Joey looked at her incredulously. "Hey, Ma, are you kidding? Mr. Cohen and the guys will kill me. This is the finals. C'mon, Ma."

Henrietta appeared in the bedroom doorway, sleepy, disheveled. "Why is everybody *shouting?* One more loud voice and I will hemorrhage, I know it. *What* is going *on?*" Her eyes grew suddenly alert as she looked at Christine. "What is it, Chris?"

Christine turned to her, trying to keep the depth of her fear out of her eyes. "It's Nick, Henrietta. He's . . . something's wrong. We've got to get out. He's gone crazy. He's . . . we can't stay here."

The front door slammed. Christine and Henrietta stood immobile, looking at one another as Nick came up the stairs. He stopped at the doorway.

"Hi, folks," he said. "Hello, Ace, got a game today? I think I'll go and watch you." His glance slid past Christine to Henrietta. "Say, Hen, old love, do we have any Band-Aids? I seem to have bumped my noggin on something."

Henrietta looked at him sharply, then walked past him toward the bathroom. As she clattered around the medicine cabinet, Nick and Christine stared at each other. Behind the smile, the calm exterior, the malignance was still there on his face. Christine looked down at the floor, her heart sinking. Henrietta came back, a Band-Aid in her hand.

"Thank you, love," Nick said. "I'd kiss you but you look particularly bad this morning." Henrietta did not smile. She gave him another long, measuring look. "C'mon, champ." Nick placed his hand on Joey's head. "Let's go warm up."

As they walked down the stairs, the tears flooded again into Christine's eyes. She sat down on the bed, her head in her hand. Henrietta walked over and stroked the blond hair softly. "It's okay, Chris," she said. "We'll manage. We'll manage."

Christine controlled herself with an effort. "No, we won't manage. We can't. We've lost. He's not crazy. It's worse. You can't imagine. They've taken him. They'll harm us. We've got to get away. You don't know what they do. You wouldn't believe . . ." Christine could not go on.

Henrietta's face broke into lines of sadness as she looked down at her distraught niece. "Perhaps I know more than you think I do, Chris. I've been doing some detective work of my own. The things I've seen would . . ."

The sound of a departing car brought them both to the window. Christine saw Joey in the front seat, his soccer ball on his lap.

"Joey!" she screamed. She ran downstairs and out the front door. She screamed her son's name again but the car was already out of sight. Christine ran into the hall to call the police. The telephone had been ripped out of the wall. The one in the kitchen had also been ripped out. She ran up the stairs to her bedroom. Next to the useless phone was a note:

Whores should not leave their houses. It's bad for business.

Christine walked unsteadily down the stairs and into the living room. She sat down on the couch, Henrietta sat down beside her.

"What can we do, Henrietta? We've got to do something." Christine realized how her voice sounded but did not care.

"Take it easy, honey," Henrietta said. "One thing I know. Nick would never harm Joey. I'm sure of it. It's just possible he took him to his game."

"I want Joey here," Christine shouted. "I want my son."

"All right, dearie," Henrietta said, after a moment's scrutiny. "I'll go get dressed and we'll go get a ride with someone to the police station. If we have to we'll walk. I won't be a minute."

"Hurry," Christine pleaded. "It's Joey, Henrietta."

She sat waiting in the living room, numb, unable to collect her thoughts. Henrietta was right. Nick would never harm Joey. They were at the game. They had to be! And then she remembered Nick that morning. The mad eyes that mirrored the demonic shadow on his soul. She heard again the demented bull bellow as he raced toward her in that unthinkable position, the crack of the broken corral railing. Wouldn't harm Joey? He had meant to harm her this morning, she was sure of it. Christine leaned back, her eyes closed, her head lolling slowly from side to side.

The knock on the front door was strong, insistent. Christine jumped up as if she had been expecting it. Joey! Nick! She ran to the door and opened it. Sleek, huge, immaculate, Karl Anderson stood before her.

23

My dear Mrs. Marino," Anderson said. "How magnificent you look this morning. I'm fortunate to have you as my neighbor to brighten my days, to illumine my nights." His hand was resting on the top of the door. Christine tried to close it. It did not move. "May I come in?" He brushed past her, walked into the living room and turned to face her. "You have no right to be so beautiful, Mrs. Marino. You are a disturber of the peace, a spoiler of tranquillity. There must be a law about it in our town ordinances, somewhere." He looked at her closely. "What's this, what's this? Tears in the morning? Name the fiend who has done this to you and I'll have his head." His face was mocking. He stared at her body in open lust.

Christine looked at him in dull hatred. "Where are they?" she said in a low voice. "Where is my son?"

Anderson shook his head. "Whatever happened to the social amenities?" he asked. He sat down, crossed his legs carefully and smiled at Christine.

"I want my son," Christine said. "Where is he?"

Anderson pretended to think. "Your son? Why he's at my house, of course. Your son and your husband are at my house. The last time I saw them, they were playing a game together. Joey's having such a splendid time, he's decided to spend the night. I'm sure you won't mind. Do you mind? Ah, good."

Christine felt faint but would not sit down. "Give him back to me. You've got Nick. You don't need Joey, too."

"Of course you'll get him back. I have no use for him. I have no use for children at all." His eyes flared momentarily. He continued to regard her with a strange, eager anticipation. "Your husband, my colleague, says you think you know all about me. Do you know all about me, Mrs. Marino?"

"I . . . I know what you are."

His expression did not change. "I sense an element of distaste. Faint, but discernible. You do not approve of me."

"Approve! Approve! You are inhuman. You are a monster who kills . . ."

"You find me unattractive."

"You murdered those two young people, you killed my dogs. You are a killer . . ."

"You find me boorish."

"You maim and you kill. You kidnapped my son. You took my husband and turned him into a horrible . . . a horrible . . ."

"Troll."

Christine felt her fear and anguish turning into hysteria, but she could not stop. "Yes, a troll, you unnatural bastard. I want my son. I want my husband back." She was sobbing now. "I want you to leave us alone." Anderson's eyes were following her every movement like a cat with a helpless fluttering bird. "Why are you doing this to us?" Christine asked softly, defeated. "Why are you so evil?"

Anderson feigned surprise. "Evil? What a strange choice of words. No one calls the lion evil as it carries away the newborn gazelle in its first breath of life. No one chastises the mantis as it placidly chews off the head of its victim. Evil? I am innocent. In this world, my dear Mrs. Marino, we are what we are." He stared at her musingly for a moment. "Or what we become."

When Christine managed to raise her eyes to look at him, she was shocked by what she saw. An intense look of longing was etched on his face. It revolted her more than anything he had ever done or said to her.

"What we become," he repeated, his voice devoid of mockery for the moment.

A fresh wave of horror jolted Christine. "What . . . what are you talking about?"

Anderson shook his head. "You have a flaw, Mrs.

Marino. You and your husband, Nicholas. A serious flaw. It is you two who brought murder to this charming neighborhood. You two who brought the mayhem."

"We've done nothing! Nothing!"

"Nothing?" His voice rolled like thunder in the room, powerful beyond belief. A glass figure on the mantelpiece trembled and then fell, shattering on the fireplace hearth. "Look in that mirror, my Christine." His voice was quiet now. He rose and walked toward her. "Look at that incredible face and tell me you've done nothing." As he stood behind her, he reached one hand up and stroked her hair, barely touching it. Christine shook under his touch. "It was you. You and your handsome husband. Oh, yes. You created . . . attractions. You aroused your sleepy, inhuman neighbors. In certain inhuman quarters, arousal brings havoc. Yes, yes, you brought havoc to Mill Harbor. You brought the whirlwind, my Christine. You shall learn to dance in it."

Christine mustered the little courage she had left and turned to face him. His hand remained stretched toward her, an extension of frozen menace. "Let us go," she beseeched him quietly, the words screaming in her brain. "Give me back my son and my husband. We'll move away. You'll never see us again. I'll say nothing, nothing."

The index finger of his outstretched hand moved back and forth slowly. "You are an unfeeling, cruel woman, Mrs. Marino. It's part of your charm. Never see me again! I find that particularly untempting. No, Christine. Your family and mine are inextricably interwoven for the next two hundred years or so. Nick and his love." His voice fell to a near whisper. "You and I. You shall learn joy, Christine, inherit ecstasy. The joys of the night, the ecstasy of my dark paradise. You, my love, and I."

Christine tried not to let the revulsion she felt show in her face. From the quick look of brutal rage that flickered across his features, she knew that she had been unsuccessful. She could not look into those eyes. She dared not move.

"Despite your pleas and entreaties to stay," he said thickly, "I have to leave now. No, no. I really have to go. Come over tomorrow around five. We'll have cocktails, a neighborly chat. We'll settle this whole unpleasant misunderstanding. I do believe Nick is graduating tomorrow. Oh, the circle of life. Someone graduates, someone enrolls. It's endless. I tell you, endless. And after that you can take Joey home. Oh, I understand that your telephones are out of order. That saves me the trouble of telling you not to use them. I want you and your aunt to stay at home until our visit tomorrow. Contact with anyone will spoil all my fun. And when I'm grouchy, I take it out on children. And I can be, oh, so grouchy. You understand." He turned to leave the room.

Tears welled again in Christine's eyes. "Karl Anderson," she said. "Don't harm my son. Please. You and your daughter. Don't . . . harm . . . my . . . son."

Anderson faced her. He was smiling. "Just don't make me grouchy and everything will be fine. Just fine." His smile widened into a cold grin. "Oh, by the way, my dear woman. I have no daughter." He opened the front door and closed it quietly behind him.

Christine stood there unmoving. Let this be a nightmare, she thought. Please, God, let me wake up. Now. She opened her eyes. Henrietta was standing at the living room entrance looking at her. The eyes of the two women met.

"Henrietta," Christine said, "I . . ."

"Sit down," Henrietta said. "Stop crying, dry your eyes. I heard him. You know I always listen to everything on the stairs. Please stop that sniffling. You'll have me doing it. We've got to think."

"Think? What about? He's most probably watching the house. We have no telephone. If we try to do anything, he'll . . . hurt Joey. He's capable of it. What is there to think about?"

"There is always something to think about, Christine. Although we do have to be careful. The man is a beast. A terrible, terrible beast. I know all about him. I told you I'd do some detective work. Well, I've been snooping on him and his daughter ever since Bowen told you how rotten he was. Yes, I heard that, too. It's all in my diary. Evil man. And his daughter is just as bad."

"He . . . he said he didn't have any daughter."

"Nonsense. She's real, all right. And she's a neurotic, evil person."

"I don't give a damn about either of them. I want my son back."

Henrietta patted her shoulder, her mouth a firm line. "And you shall have him, honey, you shall have him."

Henrietta padded up the stairs determinedly. She entered her bedroom and opened her closet door.

Something simple and dignified, she thought. She selected a pale blue dress and shoes to match. The blond wig, without the extra fall. She nodded her head. Makeup. Lots of it. Don't let it show. In half an hour she was ready. She looked in the mirror. Her glance ranged down her body, and up again to her face. She stared into the bleak eyes. The days of wine and roses, eh, kid. She walked back to her dressing table, opened a perfume bottle, poured a double shot of Scotch out of it into the top, and drank it. She sat down on the bed, wrote a hasty note, and put it on top of her diary in the middle of the pillow. A little dramatic, she thought, but what the hell.

Henrietta walked as quietly downstairs as the high heels would allow her. She saw Christine standing listlessly by the stove, the teakettle whistling unnoticed in front of her. My poor Christine, Henrietta thought. Somebody's got to do something. I'll get Joey back. Even those two creatures can be spoken to, can listen to reason. I'll insist on it.

She walked outside, closing the door softly behind her. The afternoon sun was still warm but shadows had begun to checkerboard the landscape. The air smelled of cedar and the Sound. She looked across the corral to the dark pines beyond. Anderson was nowhere in sight. This whole thing is ridiculous, she thought. She adjusted her wig and straightened her brassiere. But I'll set it right. *Maintenant!* Those creeps won't get a word in edgewise. And besides. Uncouth and weird as they are, they wouldn't hurt an old lady. She stepped across the lawn toward the indifferent trees.

24

Christine sat on the terrace staring out over the copper-colored water, a cup of cold tea held motionless in her hand. Birds flew noisily over the tree-shadowed lawn. That's the life, Christine thought. Find a seed, sing a little, and spread your wings in the sunshine. No complications. Wrong again, lady. You forgot about the cats that catch them and play with them. She shook her head. Always there are the cats.

Christine rose stiffly and walked into the kitchen. It's too damn quiet in here, she thought angrily. Without Joey life is too damn quiet. I can't be alone now. I'll go crazy. She walked up the stairs and knocked on

Henrietta's door. After waiting a moment, she opened the door and walked into the room. Henrietta was gone. An alarm sounded in Christine when she saw the note on top of the diary. She read it quickly.

Dearie,
Have gone to Andersons to straighten this whole contretemps out. Don't worry, took my hatpin.

Shall return with Joey forthwith. Have dinner ready for us. Don't botch the salad. A Beaujolais would be nice.

Au revoir,
H.

P.S. Read the diary from September first only!!! Our neighbors, no matter what you call them, are not dealing with a full deck.

P.P.S. The rest of the diary is PRIVATE!!! Filled with nuance, beauty, and the essence of what it is to be Woman. KEEP OUT!!!

Au revoir encore,
H.

Christine looked down at the note unbelievingly. Henrietta! Into that den of serpents. I've got to stop her. Ridiculous. She could have left an hour ago. Then go over to the Andersons' and get her. Impossible. This whole thing is impossible. If they've hurt her, killed her, what can you do? You can stay out of their clutches and think. You're the only one left. A small cry escaped Christine's lips. The sound of it startled her. My God, it's true. I'm the only one left. I'm alone.

They've killed my dogs, they've claimed my husband, they've taken my child, God knows what's happened to Henrietta, no telephone, no Lieutenant Broderick. My last hope is Bowen. Where the hell are you, Bowen? She sat down on the bed and breathed deeply to keep the hysteria away. Cut it out, Christine. If you break down there's no one to help Joey. No one. Sit still. Keep very still and think. Her glance darted around the room. Think? I'm lucky I still have my sanity. Her eyes fell on the diary resting on the pillow. What had Henrietta said? September first? She picked it up and turned the pages, trying not to let her hand shake.

September 1.
Played detective today. Promised Christine I would. Hid in the reeds and watched the Anderson house after dinner. Incroyable! Karla Anderson riding around in the twilight on the back of a dog. Looked more like a wolf. Used a live snake as reins. Do you believe this! I sneezed and both pair of eyes were in my direction instanter. Nearly had a lavatorial accident. Red eyes? Some neighbors Nick and Christine picked. Crazy as loons. I'd rather live next door to Hitler.

Mustn't tell Christine. She's upset enough already. Gather all the facts and give them to that good-looking lieutenant. Might wind up on the payroll.

September 2.
Don't know how to write this. Am so indignant I tremble. Stationed myself in the reeds so I could see the Andersons' pool. Nick was there. On all fours. Karla

Anderson was riding him around the pool. He had a snake in his mouth, for a bridle. I nearly fainted. Couldn't move. After a while he lay down on the grass. That woman starts rubbing him all over with some kind of oil. Crooning in his ear. Howling is more like it. Almost fainted again. Just then the master of the house comes out of the woods, stage left. He's wearing a bathing suit. Never have I seen anything so huge, so disgusting. He's holding this poor, dear struggling rabbit by the hind legs. Sits down on a lounge chair, holds the poor thing up and watches it wiggle. Cruel monster! Then he clamps his jaws on its throat. The last thing I remember before I fainted was that fat vampire sucking on that rabbit, eyes closed, face flushed. Woke up, the three of them were floating in the pool on rubber mats, drinking sodas. Lunatics, all. I threw up quietly and went home.

September 3.
Cannot go back to Hell House this morning. Simply do not have the courage. Shall stay in my room and try to forget yesterday. Perhaps read a little. Finish hook rug?

Dark out now. Little bunnies all over room. Got to protect them from Fatso!! Rabbits of the world unite!!! Good night.

September 4.
Went over there again today. Didn't think I could do it. Amazing. The whole morning was a tremendous bore. Nick, Karla, Fatso, and Maynard Drogin talking, sleeping in the sun. Everything so normal I could hardly believe my eyes. Maynard cooking steaks on a grill. Everyone drinking Bloody Marys.

Curious. When Drogin lit the charcoal lighter, the other three nearly jumped out of their chairs. Looked really scared! Weirdos afraid of fire? Interesting.

September 5.
That's it. No more snooping. Finis. My heart won't stand another day. Walked past the boathouse this afternoon on way to Andersons'. Heard howling coming from it. Took everything I had to walk up to it. Did it. Peered through a crack in the boards. Worst thing I ever saw. Nick, naked as a jaybird, covered with some kind of slime. He's being held up in the air by Karla and her father. They each have an arm and a leg and they're pulling on them. How strong that girl must be. They're both leaning over and howling in his ear. I refused to faint again. After I don't know how many minutes of this, they put him down. Anderson went over to a bag in the corner and takes out another rabbit. He hands the little darling to Nick. Backed away until my knees gave out. Knelt right there and prayed for Nick. Prayed for us all. Our neighbors are insane. Dr. Stirner was right. They are not human. Shall inform Lieutenant Broderick of this first chance I get. Lock them up and throw away the key.

September 6.
Too tired to write. Christine sold five paintings today. She was so proud. Saw that terrible man and his daughter. Shall type up what I know about them and deliver it to the police pronto. They should not be walking around among decent people. Fearsome couple. Terrible eyes. I shall see them in my dreams.

Christine put the diary down and looked at it. She

sat that way for a long time, her face drawn, her eyes brimming with fresh tears. Poor Nick, she thought, my poor Nick. Poor Henrietta, and Joey. My God, Joey.

She blinked her eyes several times, spilling her tears, and sat up straight. Come *on*, lady. The serpents have taken everything you love in this world. Fight them. Kill them. *Do* something.

Christine rose and walked slowly into her bedroom. She pulled a chair over to the window and sat down, peering into the deepening night. No Henrietta. No Joey. She glanced at the clock. It was eight o'clock. Do something. While you're waiting, stop crying and think. There must be something. A key. Everyone has a weakness, even the serpents.

Bowen! There was a word, a phrase she had read in Henrietta's diary tonight that had echoed something from Bowen's report. She closed her eyes. There was something . . . something. She tried to concentrate but it was no use. Her brain was filled with a whining, malicious, elfin voice.

"She's not coming back, you know. Henrietta's gone. Maybe she's dead. Maybe she'll burst through your window tonight, howling, lusting for blood. The bastard magic is quick, powerful. Poor Christine. So alone."

Christine put her hands over her ears. She saw the movement of her arms in the mirror above her dressing table. She stared at herself, unbelieving. The dark-circled, wild eyes, the fearful expression that creased her face. Who the hell is that? she thought. Okay, Christine, calm down. Just . . . calm . . . down. She gazed at herself steadily in the mirror, trying to restore some semblance of balance to her distraught features. She was not too successful. Hey, Christine—she watched her lips mouth the words—you break down and there are no more good guys. Nobody left even to keep score.

She stood up, clicked the lights off and returned to her chair. She sat motionless in the darkened room, staring out the window toward the tall pine trees that led to the Anderson house. She tried to will the figures of Henrietta and Joey to appear, but there was only the empty, moonlit path. It was eleven o'clock when she finally stood up again and walked over to the closet for her sweater. She never put it on. He'll hurt Joey if he sees me leave the house. The maniac-beast is watching, I know it. He'll hurt my son. Christine fell on her bed in frustration and exhaustion. Without wanting to, she fell into an uneasy sleep.

Christine dreamed. She dreamed of a beautiful park. It was autumn. Red and gold leaves flamed in the sun. Couples strolled along the leaf-strewn paths in dignified slow motion. They were dressed in nineteenth-century clothing, with bonnets, canes, parasols. There was a château in the background. Beautiful music was coming from somewhere.

A gentle wind stirred the bright leaves, setting visual fire to the landscape. One tree, a yellow and bronze willow, shook violently, then rose from the ground. The leaves turned into the flowing golden curls of a young giant shaking his head, awakening from sleep. He stretched, yawned, and rose up on one elbow. His face was coarse, beardless, beautiful.

The couples kept up their slow, mechanical walking,

paying no attention to the huge, burnished body that framed their horizon. The giant followed them idly with his eyes for a moment and then, seeming to tire, he opened his mouth and emitted a shattering roar. Myriad leaves scurried in the air, women held their skirts, men chased their straw hats. Some of the women giggled at the broken parasols; annoyance appeared on the faces of several of the men. Still no one looked up. As the giant opened his mouth to roar again, huge gobs of blood drooled out of his mouth like saliva. Upon seeing this, the women looked up and began to exclaim, "Oh, there's a troll, he's a troll, look, a troll, do you see the troll, a troll, a troll." They gathered in front of the huge head, pointing excitedly, murmuring the word over and over again.

A look of brute malignance spread over the giant features. His lips drew back revealing two long teeth protruding upward from his lower jaw. He reached down into the milling crowd in front of him and picked up a young boy by the arm, who struggled and screamed in his grasp. Reaching over with his other hand, the giant held each of the boy's arms in his fingertips. His eyes had the cruel look of a bored, insane prisoner holding a helpless fly.

Christine awoke with a feeling of horror so intense that she could not catch her breath. She was soaked with perspiration. She sat up and shook her head, trying to clear her sleep-fogged brain. She was fully awake now, but the horror persisted. She walked over to the chair by the window and sat down, afraid to close her eyes, to dream again. She stared into the darkness before her, trembling, waiting for the dawn.

25

*H*enrietta stood in the Andersons' driveway looking at the huge, tree-darkened house. Not a very desirable neighbor, she decided, noting the storm windows lying around, the crooked shutters, the dead branches on the roof and scattered in the long lawn grass. There was something about the house that made her pause irresolutely where she was for several long moments. Once, she turned to go back, but the thought of Joey in that evil-looking house made up her mind. She walked up to the door and rapped the heavy metal knocker against it several times.

"It's open, Mrs. Knapp."

Startled, Henrietta turned toward the voice behind

her. Karl Anderson was standing in the driveway, his hands in his jacket pockets, his face unreadable. He *had* been watching the house, Henrietta realized.

"I am under the impression that you and Mrs. Marino were to remain at home tonight. Is it possible she didn't tell you?" His voice was polite, but it had an underlying quality that made Henrietta look at him closely.

"Oh, yes. Yes, she told me. It's just that I thought you and I could discuss this thing civilly. I mean about Joey being here. And everything." She did not like the timbre of her voice.

"It was not very wise of you, Mrs. Knapp. I will assume that Mrs. Marino will not be equally foolish."

"Oh, of course not, Christine is at home. She's staying right there." I sound like a frightened little girl, she admonished herself. She pulled herself erect. "May we go inside and talk?" He gestured toward the door and followed her in.

Henrietta glanced around the interior of the house. Just like the outside, she thought. Beautiful decadence. Large rooms with high ceilings. Finely carved furniture, dusty, frayed. Several large mirrors, filmed and cracked. One actually had a cobweb in one corner. No rugs, no ornaments, no pictures, nothing on the faded walls except a large mounted elk horn. There was no softness anywhere, no warmth.

"I love your house," she said. "I've never seen anything like it before."

Anderson stood leaning against the coiled end of the banister, looking at her. His eyes made her uncomfortable.

"Really lovely," she said. Get this over with, she told herself, and get out of here. "Mr. Anderson, I came over here to talk to you about Joey. I really think he should come home with me now. He's not used to sleeping in strange beds. Where is he, by the way?"

"I believe he's upstairs with his father, watching television."

"May I see him?"

"No."

Henrietta's eyes flared. "You know, you have no right to do this. If you persist we shall be forced to file a very serious charge against you. The police, including my very dear friend Lieutenant Broderick, would be very interested . . ." She stopped. Mrs. Anderson had appeared at the top of the stairs. After a pause, she walked silently down the stairs toward them. She halted just above Anderson and both of them stood, unmoving, looking at Henrietta. For the first time that night, Henrietta felt the faint pricklings of fear.

Without changing his stare, Anderson spoke. "Mrs. Knapp was just telling me, Mama, about going to the police. Mrs. Knapp has friends in the police department." Mrs. Anderson's face did not change, but something came into her eyes that forced Henrietta to look away.

"I was only saying, Mrs. Anderson, that I think the boy would be better off spending the night in his own home. I'm sure you'll understand." She tried a tentative smile. There was no response from the other woman. Henrietta faltered before the two sets of unblinking eyes. Was there a reddish glow deep within them or was it her imagination? "Actually, there's no need for the police," she said. "Just let me have the boy and I'm sure Mrs. Marino will forget the whole . . . misunderstanding." There was still no response. What a pair, she thought. It's like negotiating with two snakes. "As a matter of fact," she attempted a smile once more, "I'm pretty sure I can get Mrs. Marino to think about moving away from here. I mean, when two neighbors can't seem to get along, the sensible thing is to . . ." She saw Anderson's eyebrows go up in mock surprise. That bastard is playing with me, she thought. Be calm, Henrietta. Stay calm. "Well, you do have, shall we say, an alternate life-style that is incompatible with Mrs. Marino's and her son's, so it would seem reasonable . . ."

"'Alternate life-style'?" The hint of a smile played around Anderson's mouth. "Whatever are you talking about, Mrs. Knapp?"

Henrietta could contain herself no longer. "I've seen you, Anderson. I know what you do. Does your mother know that you kill harmless rabbits? Does she? What I'm saying, troll, witch, or whatever it is that you are, is give me the boy and we'll get out of your life. We won't say anything to anybody. Just give us the boy." Oh, my, she thought. You made a bad mistake, Henrietta. She had seen his reaction when she had mentioned the word "troll." I think you made a bad mistake, old girl.

In the silence that followed, Mrs. Anderson walked down the final few stairs and approached Henrietta. The two women stood facing each other, wordless, unmoving. As Henrietta stared into the bright blue eyes, Mrs. Anderson raised her arms and placed her fingers lightly on Henrietta's temples. In fear and annoyance, Henrietta brushed at the outstretched arms with her hand. The arms did not move. It was as if they were welded in place. A flash of pure terror raced through Henrietta. The rapt fingers probed her eyelids now. This is an indignity, Henrietta shouted to herself, trying to keep her body from shaking. She felt her throat being touched, pressed gently. After what seemed an eternity, the fingers disappeared.

"Good-bye, Mrs. Knapp." It was Anderson speaking. "It is time for you to go to sleep."

Henrietta thought for a moment about calling Joey's name, but the menace in the room was so heavy she did not want him near it. I'll go to the police, she thought. It's the only thing I can do.

She walked as steadily as she could and heard the door close behind her. She had taken several steps before she heard the door open again. Looking back she saw Mrs. Anderson framed by the light in the doorway. A fresh wave of fear swept through Henrietta, and she turned and hurried her steps. Knowing she was being watched, she decided to go back to the house and speak to Christine. She started across the uncut lawn. In another moment she felt the presence of someone walking along beside her. Although she knew it was impossible for anyone to move that fast, Henrietta turned her head. There, walking at her side, matching her stride for stride, was Mrs. Anderson, her eyes gleaming in the darkness. Henrietta was about to say something to her but the expression on the old woman's face froze the words on her lips. She increased her pace, but the old woman remained silently by her side. Henrietta began to run. One of her high heels broke off, but she continued to run, panting heavily. The old woman, whose long gray hair had become unfastened, stayed at her shoulder, imitating her hobbling gait, moving effortlessly. Exhausted, Henrietta fell to the ground. Looking up she saw the figure of the other woman standing immobile, her hands at her sides, her face turned toward the star-filled sky. Painfully, Henrietta rose, terror driving her forward. As they neared the trees at the end of the lawn, Henrietta felt her shoulder grasped in an immutable grip. She screamed and turned to face her assailant. The horrific figure she saw beside her drained the blood from her face. She fainted. She did not feel the fingers penetrate her flesh or the bones crack as the hand raised her high into the moon-bright sky, saluting the heavens in an ancient and sinister silhouette.

26

The next afternoon, as Christine walked along the shore path toward the Anderson house, it took all the courage she could muster just to keep her shoulders straight. I've got to do this and do it well, she told herself. I've got to get Joey out of this nightmare, now. She was badly shaken by the events of the previous day: Joey's abduction, Anderson's visit, that awful, unforgettable dream. And Henrietta had not returned. Henrietta was gone. The nightmare would not end.

As she walked across the lawn toward the house, Christine's heart leaped. She almost cried for joy. Near the overgrown patio, trying listlessly to kick a soccer ball through the tall grass, was Joey, still in his soccer uniform. Christine ran to him and flung her arms around him. She would not let him go. Joey returned the embrace. His body began to shake with sobs he could no longer repress. Christine had the sudden impulse to flee, to stand up and run away with Joey that instant. Over the shoulder of her trembling son she saw Nick and Karl Anderson standing in the doorway that led from the patio. They were both motionless, staring at her expectantly like two jungle cats whose prey has suddenly lifted its head. Her eyes met Anderson's evenly. I've got Joey, she thought. You'll have to kill me, troll-bastard, to get him back.

Anderson walked through the grass toward her. There was triumph in his eyes. "Mrs. Marino. How truly wonderful it is when neighbors come to call. How about a martini? I've had several. They're quite crisp."

Christine stood up. "I have what I want, Anderson," she said.

"Lucky, lucky Mrs. Marino," Anderson commented sardonically. "A truly enviable position. I can only try to emulate you." He smiled and reached for Joey's shoulder. The boy recoiled into his mother's arms, away from the huge, outstretched hand.

As Christine held her son tightly to her, she was watching Nick. His reaction had startled her. When Anderson had reached toward Joey, Nick's eyes had rolled and widened. His head had begun to shake back and forth like a malfunctioning robot. As Christine watched him, a sudden realization swept through her. It's Joey. My God. It's Joey. They haven't been able to destroy that bond yet. Not all of it. It's Joey, Joey is the key. With renewed strength, she turned to Anderson. "My son doesn't want you to touch him, Anderson. Neither do I." She glared at him with a hatred so deep it contorted her features.

"I wouldn't dream of it, dear lady," he said. "I may be guilty of many things, but imperfect timing is not one of them."

"By the way, Anderson," Christine said flatly. "I believe my Aunt Henrietta paid you a visit last night. She didn't come home. I'd like to take her with me. Now."

"Ah, yes. Henrietta. A charming woman. So knowledgeable. She and my mother made a perfect pair."

"Where is she?" Christine demanded.

"Well, the fact is that she got hurt on the way back to your house last night. Was it her shoulder? Yes. Nasty business. We had to . . . put her to bed for the night." He smiled at her in private amusement.

"I want to see her now." Christine tried to keep the desperation out of her voice.

"Do you really?" Anderson looked at her calculatingly, his head to one side. "And so you shall." He reached into his pocket and handed Christine a key. "She's waiting for you in the boathouse, Mrs Marino. It's sort of a ritual we have around here."

"The boathouse?" Christine's eyes were alert, fearful. "I don't understand."

"And I grow impatient. And the martinis are diluting. Go, dear woman. We have so much to talk about, so much to do."

Christine started down the lawn toward the boat-house, Joey's wrist held firmly in her grasp. As she approached the shoreline, the large building loomed at her from the orange afternoon sky. Her mind raced wildly. Fear and hope, and a rising sense of terrible expectancy shattered her thoughts like an incessant crashing of breaking crystal. She halted several yards from the boathouse and looked up at the carved wooden faces, the boarded windows. A sense of deep foreboding filled her being.

Christine began to walk around the building toward the entrance. She ran her fingers along the rough, faded wood. Compose your thoughts, she told herself, compose your thoughts. Her mind would not compose. Instead, like the first gentle winds of a distant hurricane, she heard faint noises, voices. Dimly at first, then growing louder and louder. Ancient horns trumpeted down to her, muted by the eons; a soft clash of arms; the whispered cries of spear-pierced horses. Louder, she heard a howl from a single throat, so powerful that it bent and cracked entire forests as it rushed toward her. She closed her eyes to the thunder of a thousand bulls, large as houses, as they bellowed and stamped in titanic rutting. And then she heard a single siren voice singing her name. Singing with such beauty that Christine felt a sudden joy swell within her. The voice was joined by a hundred others and then a hundred more, until she felt her heart and mind would burst with ecstasy.

"Hey, Mom, you all right?" Her son's small voice

dispelled the sweet tumult that had been echoing in Christine's head.

Bewildered, she looked down at Joey. "Yes," she said. "I'm all right now." She looked up at the massive door before her.Without knowing why, she said, "Joey, wait for me here. Don't move. I'll be right back."

With trembling fingers she unlocked the boathouse door and flung it open.

A shaft of sunlight penetrated the black interior. Christine stepped inside, her eyes narrowing in the sudden darkness. And then she saw it. Illuminated by the light from the doorway, a figure lay spread in the shadowy light. It was Henrietta. Her wrists and ankles were tightly strapped to the four corners of a huge, flat stone. Her head hung down over its edge in mute, terrible bondage. Blood from a jagged bone protruding from one shoulder was caked on the tightly arched neck and had dripped onto the artificial yellow curls that stretched downward to the ground. Unseeing, upside-down eyes stared into Christine's unbelieving gaze.

Christine opened her mouth to scream. Unstoppable rushes of mindless terror surged out of her throat in steady spasms. They continued unchecked, soundless, shaking her whole body.

The screech of ripping nails and tearing wood came from beyond where Henrietta lay. The face of Karl Anderson appeared, framed in the open window. His eyes glowed redly. His face was creased in a wild, triumphant smile. His mouth opened wide in horrific imitation of Christine's agony. His head moved from side to side like a lion in a silent dream, prowling a nightmare savanna. And then a low roar emanated from his throat. It grew in volume until it became an unbearable alien bellow, filling the room with madness. Christine's eyes fluttered. She fell senseless to the ground, as the abominable sound echoed and reechoed among the high, hidden rafters.

27

Seated on a couch in the Anderson living room, Christine watched the fog roll off the Sound through a large dust-covered window. It crept across the bay toward the house in gradually thickening billows, merging with the dark cedars and then engulfing them. She remembered clearly what had happened: awakening in Karl Anderson's arms as he carried her across the lawn; the fear and the terrible weakness that left her unable to struggle; Joey's tight grasp on her hand that kept her from fainting again. And then she remembered something else. The love-lorn look her opening eyes had caught on Anderson's face as he held her. Nightmares are like that, Christine thought dully. Deeper and deeper into the dark forest. And who's always waiting at Grandmother's house? She tightened her arm around Joey seated on the couch beside her. Her free hand smoothed his hair absently as she continued to stare out at the fog.

Christine knew Nick was in the room. Her glance had caught him briefly, seated in the darkness of a far corner. She had not looked at him again, fearing what his face would tell her. And yet, she had to know. There might not be that much time. Slowly, her eyes left the window. She gazed at the carved woodwork around the ceiling, the huge mantelpiece above the fireplace, the sparse, expensive furniture. Deer horns and stuffed birds hung here and there on the walls, and there were ancient, musty drapes around the high windows. Dust was everywhere. Spiderwebs patterned the corners. Her gaze finally fell on Nick. He was looking at Joey, his eyes heavy-lidded, inscrutable. He was holding a drink in both hands in front of his face. Christine tried to pierce that terrible, enchanted armor with a look of love and pain, but his expression did not change. Unable to bear what she saw in his face, Christine turned her head toward the window again and looked hopelessly into the oncoming mist.

Karl Anderson came back into the room and stood in front of Christine. Her eyes closed involuntarily. "Anyone for martinis?" he said brightly. "Mrs. Marino?" He placed a silver tray on the table in front of her. "Did you say olive or lemon twist?"

Christine's eyes remained shut. "I don't drink with

murderers," she said quietly. She could not look at him.

"I don't know why not," Anderson said, unruffled. "I make a very good martini."

Christine bit her lip. The memory of Henrietta crashed before her eyes. Don't cry in front of him, she thought. Don't cry.

"I'm going to pour you one anyway," Anderson said. "Call it a celebration. Your aunt is not dead, my dear."

Christine opened her eyes, her face livid. "Liar!" her voice exploded. "I saw her! Liar!"

Anderson's face remained impassive. "Did you say olive? Excellent choice." He sat heavily in a chair opposite her, settling himself comfortably with drink in hand. He smiled, masking a deeper exultation. "You wound me deeply, Christine. You know how sensitive I am." He sipped his drink, still smiling. "I speak the truth, dear lady. Your aunt is still alive. She is not in the best condition imaginable, but then, who of us really is." He raised his glass to his lips again and leaned back in the chair. "Unjust, beautiful Christine. It was not I, sweet lady, who attacked your aunt."

Something screamed in the recesses of Christine's mind. Nick! Dear God, no!

"Oh, I would have," Anderson continued, stirring the ice with his finger. "We trolls do that. But your aunt wasn't mine. It was my mother, my dear Mrs. Marino, who did the nasty deed." Anderson's eyes feasted on Christine's astonishment and horror. "A wedding present to herself on this nuptial night of nights. Don't look at me that way. It's in all the marriage guides. Each new husband and wife must learn to sacrifice . . ." The smile grew wider. "And after all, dear woman, what is a wedding without something old . . ." His eyes flickered across Joey for an instant as he took another drink. "Something new." As Christine sat in mounting horror, the fierce eyes returned to her face. "I've surprised you. Is it about Mama? Did you really believe, Christine Marino, that I could be a troll and my mother be anything else? You are beautiful, my dear, but not very perceptive."

Hardly able to speak, Christine whispered, "And your daughter? She's . . . one . . . too?"

Anderson shook his huge head patiently. "Christine, Christine. What am I going to do with you?" He took a long drink as he stared at her. "What am I *ever* going to do with you? I told you yesterday. I see it bears repetition. I have no daughter."

"But Karla. You told me she was your daughter."

"I lied." Anderson leaned back, using his free hand expansively. "You have no idea how the lack of a Judeo-Christian ethic frees one so completely. You ought to try it sometime." He glanced back at Nick, who looked down at his lap. Christine had the feeling that a joke had passed between them. "Yes, maybe I can be of some service there. But I digress. No, Karla is not my daughter. Because you see, dear lady, Karla is my mother."

Christine found it difficult to breathe. Pieces of a horrible jigsaw puzzle tumbled about in her mind. Bowen's report. Mrs. Anderson's intense attachment to

Nick. Never seeing Karla and Mrs. Anderson together. Christine's mind reeled.

Anderson finished his drink and poured himself another. His swollen features gleamed in the eerie foglight from the window. "In view of the imminent . . . involvement . . . of our two families," he said, "I feel that I owe you some explanation. It's all quite simple, really. As I've told you, my mother, precious dear, is a troll. Unlike myself, however, she is a throwback. Her appearance is not as . . . socially acceptable as my own. Ah, the vicissitudes of the chromosomes. But it has its compensations. Because she is a throwback she has retained an ancient art. The ability to transform oneself, to assume a more pleasant shape. Some days it was Karla. That was for your husband. Mostly it was little, perfect Mama."

Despite herself, Christine was listening as he spoke. She remembered how she had been struck by the perfection in the faces of the two women. It had been a damned murdering troll's conception of what these women should look like, she thought.

Anderson took another drink. "An ancient, wonderful art," he said. "How I wish that I could do it. Why"— his eyes leveled into Christine's—"I could even look like Bowen Stirner." The sophisticated mask crumbled slightly. "Would you love me then, Christine? Would you kiss me in thunder, in lightning light?" His hand clenched and unclenched. "But I am precipitate. And I digress precipitately." He closed his eyes and tapped his forehead with his forefinger.

Shaken, Christine turned her head toward the window. Oh my God, she thought. Oh my God. He loves me. The beast who kills is in love with me. I am loved. The realization of this, its supreme, utter absurdity, was terrifying.

The civilized veneer had returned to Anderson's face. "In order for you, my dear, to successfully go where you are going, it is necessary for you to know where we, all of us, have been. It will suit my purpose better to begin at the beginning. It's your typical troll meets girl, troll loses girl, troll gets girl story. I guess you can say that it really started with the Levines' horse. I've told Mama a hundred times to do her hunting away from the house. But when the blood lust strikes her, well, you know Mama. Then the Marinos moved in. The beautiful Marinos. And all hell broke loose. I told you last night. You are too beautiful, both of you. You upset the delicate balance we had established in this community over the past few years. From the moment Mama saw Nick from the upstairs window that first time you came to our house, his fate was decided. She wanted to take him that night in instant consummation. He would have died in the process, of course. It was I, Mrs. Marino, who convinced her that trolldom for your husband was the only way to produce a more permanent and satisfying relationship that may last months, even years. Oh, yes, Christine, your husband is a troll, make no mistake about that. Save your fleeting glances, your false hopes. Nick is with us now. Do you remember how Mama came down to the party and hung on Nick's arm? You almost didn't get him back that night. I had to send her on a quiet walk just to calm her. That's when your little dog got killed. Sheer sexual exuberance on her part. What a little tussle we had that night after everyone left. The house shook, I tell you. I saved all of your lives that evening, you can be sure. No, don't thank me. Time enough for that later.

"The next day, Mama transformed herself into 'my daughter,' Karla. I never realized just how good Mama was until I saw Karla. Exquisite workmanship. Even then your husband resisted us. Never has anyone given us so much difficulty. That difficulty is a tribute to your beauty, Christine, to your powers to evoke love and desire." Christine shivered at his smile. Her arm tightened around Joey. "You do have them, you know," he said. "No one, however, not even your stubborn Nick can withstand our magic, the siren melody. Once enchanted, defenses down, he was ours. I told you last night that it was you who caused those two teenagers to die. It was, you know. Do you remember the day you came to our pool and took Nick away from Mama-Karla? I saw the look on her face from a window. I don't know what you said to her, but I've rarely seen her like that. I won't tell you what she did for the next few hours, but when she left the house, it was impossible for me to stop her. I knew our community would never be quite the same. Fortunately, she had the wit to travel to and from the carnage as little, old Mama. Why, the police even gave her a ride home, telling her she shouldn't be out walking so late at night. An angry troll is not a nice troll. A jealous troll is, to the fullest sense of that word, disagreeable." He paused. His eyes looked steadily into Christine's. "Bowen Stirner would know what I mean," he added quietly.

Christine's eyes narrowed as she stared at the brutish face. "Bowen Stirner knows all about you. He'll find us gone. I'm surprised he's not here with the police already."

Anderson's eyes roamed over her like a questing, insistent hand. "I think not," he said.

Seeing his face, Christine turned toward the window again. He seems so sure of himself, she thought. Oh God, has something happened to Bowen? The question shrieked in her mind.

"But let us continue," said Anderson. "We shall get to the eminent professor in good time. In good time." He poured himself another drink from the pitcher on the table in front of him. "Needless to say, I was very angry with Mama. I did not want to move again. Away from you. Then, good fortune. Everyone was blaming Steinmetz. Crazy, harmless Charlie Steinmetz, and I thought everything would pass over our heads. The party at the beach ended these fancies. Your stubborn, faithful husband, fighting us, resisting us. Useless heroics. One does not resist our ancient call. One submits. But impatient Mama-Karla sings her siren song for all the world to hear. And that poem. From the ice mountains at the edge of the world. Beautiful, but blatant, so obvious to the discerning listener. One might as well buy troll T-shirts. Did you see how disturbed the handsome professor became? Did you see the look on his face? I did, you can be sure. That look plus other . . . indiscretions helped to seal his unimportant fate."

Christine swallowed hard. She didn't want to hear this. If only she could stop him. But she could not.

"And later, you, Christine, little catalyst that you are, chose to lie on the beach with your perfect, delicious breasts exposed to the pink clouds. I saw you swimming and left my little gathering just to watch you shimmer in the water like a risen nymph. Crazy, harmful Karl Anderson. Standing in the reeds, worshiping your sunset-tinted body. Sighing over those delectable mounds of joy. And then your dog attacked me. Foolish beast. Can dogs smell desire? I must have stunk with it. What was I to do? Let him bite me?" Anderson finished his drink and poured himself another, splashing the tray with an unsteady hand.

Although she tried not to show it, Christine had begun to shake, her whole body shivering uncontrollably. For the first time she noticed another sound besides Anderson's voice. In the room above them, someone had begun pacing back and forth steadily, with a tread so heavy the ceiling trembled. She heard Anderson's voice again.

"Which brings us up to the eminent professor. Oh, I saw you two. A sweet kiss in the rain. Bad professor. Bad Christine. And I, standing in the boathouse, with my poor rabbit. Pale nourishment compared to what his lips tasted that night. My dear Christine, when you kissed him you killed him. I've told you about jealous trolls. Rarely have I been more disagreeable."

Christine turned to face him, her hand to her mouth,

the awful truth rising within her. Her eyes were wide with terror. "Bowen?" She could barely speak. "You've killed Bowen? Because of me?"

Anderson's features swelled with sudden rage. His hissing answer filled the room. "Yes, I've killed your Bowen." He spat out the last word. "He was the only one who could even begin to conceive what we are in this house. And because he touched what is mine." His voice became quieter, almost subdued. "You are mine now, Christine. I've waited long enough."

Christine no longer heard his words. Instinctively, she hugged Joey closer to her. Her head was shaking back and forth in anguish and disbelief. Her dazed eyes focused on nothing.

Anderson's eyes rolled toward her. He was drunk now. "You mentioned the police before. The police will find nothing. The eminent poacher lies beneath the cement floor of the boathouse. Your aunt will join him there this night. It is three feet thick. I can lift it. They cannot. We've done it before. They will not rest alone."

Christine's will broke. Quiet sobs convulsed her body. She covered her face with her hands. "Murderer," she whispered. "Murderer. You murderer."

Anderson looked at her, one eyebrow raised. "As I told you last night, dear woman, it depends upon your point of view. We are what we are. We do what we do. And we're not as bad as you think. The blood lust is very strong, as you shall soon find out. Mama and I have graciously sublimated our desires by the use of animals. Oh, I'll admit there has been a baby here, a child there . . ." His voice trailed away.

Christine's head snapped up. Fear, like a sudden

stab of pain, stiffened her body. Anderson's gaze was resting on Joey. Christine's grip around Joey's shoulders tightened involuntarily, bringing a slight smile to Anderson's lips. Her eyes hardened in protective rage.

In the far corner of the room, Nick put his glass down quietly. Beyond Anderson's hulking shoulders, Christine watched as his head began to move back and forth, slowly at first, and then more rapidly. Suddenly, Christine remembered Nick's reaction when Anderson had reached out his hand toward Joey. She had seen it then, she saw it now. It was Joey! Joey was the key to Nick! Use it. Fight this murderer. Don't die without a fight, Christine.

Suppressing a fear that threatened to destroy her, Christine looked at Anderson again. "I see you're looking at my son, Anderson." She could hardly get the words out. "What are your plans for my son, Anderson?"

The huge man tapped his nose thoughtfully. "He presents a problem, that boy. Creatures of our ilk do not like children. Not one bit. Of course he could go into training with his mother, but, to be perfectly frank, we have very little success with children. I don't understand why. Perhaps they can't comprehend the delicate intricacies of our creed. Yes, I'd say that Joey, here, definitely presents a problem."

Out of the corner of her eye Christine was watching Nick. His face was in agony now, his body rigid. His head was still moving from left to right but his face was lifted toward the ceiling. Only the whites of his eyes were showing.

Christine's face betrayed nothing as she spoke, but

her voice was unsteady. "A problem? My son presents a problem?" She could not keep the quaver out of her voice. She knew his sudden anger, the calculated risk she was taking. She had no choice. "To a man who has . . . has killed 'a baby here, a child there'? There's nothing worse than an indecisive murderer. Make up your mind, Anderson."

His eyes looked at her in surprise and admiration. "What spirit. You shall make a perfect partner. Now that you have pressed the point, I guess your son will be . . . 'a child there.'"

"No—o—o." A long, drawn-out cry, wrenched from the depths of Nick's being, startled both of them. It was repeated louder, stronger. A fierce look of hope came, unbidden, to Christine's face. Anderson's eyes looked into hers for a brief moment before he turned toward Nick.

"Christine!" Nick's voice sounded strange, as if he were talking to her from inside a dream. "Christine! Run! Run, Christine. Joey! He'll kill him! He'll kill my son!"

Anderson's head swiveled from Nick to Christine in reptilian menace. His whole body tensed, a malevolent force ready to strike. "If you move, Mrs. Marino," he hissed. "If you move. By the time you stand up, the head of your son will roll off your lap." The absolute malignant power of the man in front of her froze Christine more than the terrific impact of his words. What am I fighting, she thought. I cannot win.

Nick was standing now, his hands clenching and unclenching. In her anguish, Christine looked at him.

And then she saw it. It was Nick! He had broken through the monstrous shroud they had woven for him, like rising through uncountable fathoms of putrescent water into the clear sunshine. It was Nick, her Nick. She saw it in his face. She saw it in his eyes, clear now, angry as hell. Christine almost smiled. If we're going to die, she thought, at least it will be the three of us, together.

Anderson was watching Nick as a diner might watch a fly struggling in his coffee. When he spoke, it was to Christine. "How very clever of you, Christine, and yet how tedious. You try my patience. All that work. Ah, well. There are quicker methods. I shall now have to slit the lens of his right eye and scratch his left eye so that he can see properly as a troll again. He'll be back with us in a matter of days. It's better for him, believe me. As a troll, he could service Mama for years, provided her appetites didn't get out of hand. You should have left him alone, Christine." He pointed to the ceiling. The heavy pacing had never stopped. He smiled at Christine's expression, looked upward with her. "Mama," he said. "You really should have left him alone. It may be impossible for me to postpone the nuptials. Tonight, as a human, his chances for survival are . . ." He shrugged his shoulders.

Nick had not moved from the corner of the room. His voice came to them, strong, controlled. "Let my son go, Anderson."

Anderson's gaze remained on Christine. "Did you hear that, my dear? The voice of the parent is heard in the land. How very clever you are, Christine. What a pair we shall make. We'll be inseparable, unstoppable. I am in awe. Paternal devotion. Of course! I should have been more careful. Love breeds carelessness, you see. Our little web had an imperfection. I must remember to be a very careful spider with you, my dear. There must be no . . ."

Nick's voice came to them like a wire about to snap. "Let my wife and child go, bastard."

Anderson did not acknowledge him. "No mistakes this time." He looked at Joey. "No imperfections."

Christine did not see Nick hurtle across the room. She saw Anderson stand up and catch Nick's lunging fist in his great hand. She heard the crack of bones as Nick's hand was crushed in that giant grip. She watched helplessly as her husband stood face to face with the huge man, his mouth drawn in pain.

"Bastard," Nick said evenly, his eyes as fierce as his captor's.

"Tedious man," Anderson said, punctuating his words by flicking the forefinger of his free hand against Nick's collarbone. Again the crack of breaking bone reached Christine's unwilling ears. She watched as the blood drained out of her husband's face, his knees almost buckling beneath him. But Nick's eyes had hardly blinked.

"Bastard," he repeated.

Anderson gripped him by the shoulder and flung him across the room as if he were a doll. Nick landed in front of the fireplace, tried to rise once, and then lay still, his eyes open.

Christine rose without a sound and went to him,

Joey's thin wrist still clutched in her hand. She knelt beside him and stroked his head. Their eyes met.

"I can't fight him, Chris," he said. "I'm sorry."

Biting her lower lip, Christine shook her head slowly to tell him it didn't matter now. Joey stared down at his father's pain-wracked face. Tears streamed down his cheeks. Suddenly, he broke from Christine's grasp and ran toward Anderson. His small fists beat on a massive arm in silent rage. Horrified, Christine screamed. "Joey! Come back here, Joey!"

Anderson looked down at the boy with distaste, holding his drink above the flailing fists. "*Go* to your mother, little boy," he said. "I find all this familial devotion tedious, most tedious. You shall all succeed in putting me in a disagreeable mood if this continues."

Christine ran across the room and pulled Joey back to where Nick was lying. She glared at Anderson, who had returned to his chair. "If I had a gun, Anderson," she said through clenched teeth, "I would shoot you. I wouldn't even watch where you fell."

Anderson was pouring himself another drink, a pained expression on his face. "Injustice," he said. "Prejudice toward trolls. You saw it. I was attacked. I merely acted in self-defense." He smiled and sipped at his drink. "I don't fear your toys, Christine. Shoot away, heartless woman. We are magical creatures, you know. There are so few things we fear on earth. So few."

Christine looked into the fireplace in rage and helplessness. Something stirred far back in her mind, something that had eluded her last night. Bowen's report. Something that trolls were afraid of. Few things on earth, I fear. There *was* something. The fireplace. Henrietta's diary! Weirdos afraid of fire! Fire! Fire! That was it! Give the beast some fire. Christine's mind raced. How? How? She had a cigarette lighter in her purse. Ridiculous. Try. Use it. Burn the beast. And if you're wrong? You have nothing to lose. I won't live without my husband, without my child. He plans to kill them. Burn the beast.

Christine leaned her head down to Joey. "Stay here," she whispered. "Stay by Daddy." Joey nodded his head. She stood up and returned to the couch, trying to adjust her face. She sat down opposite Anderson and shook her head. "Karl," she said. The name stuck in her throat like rancid vomit. "Karl, this is ridiculous. Let them go. It's me that you want. We both know that. Why hurt them?"

Anderson looked up from his drink, wary but still smiling. "What's this? What's this? Conversation from Christine? Oh, how clever you are. I know what you're doing, devious woman. You're biding your time until you can get a gun. Where is it? In your purse?"

Christine reached for her handbag and opened it. "As a matter of fact, yes," she said. Anderson's face did not change. She rummaged around in the bag and withdrew her cigarettes and lighter. "It seems I don't have a gun," she said. "I don't think I could hit you, anyway. I'm a little nervous. I need a cigarette."

Anderson's eyes were on the lighter. "Terrible habit," he said, his smile thinning.

As Christine pressed her lighter into flame, she glanced at Anderson. It was true! Bowen and Henrietta had been right! His head had indeed recoiled, his upper lip had curled with some deep, unbidden revulsion. Christine snapped the lighter shut and exhaled slowly. "You've won, Karl," she said. "Let them go. I'll do anything you want, only let them go."

Anderson shook his head, pointing to the ceiling. The pacing was quicker now. The room shook with it. "Your husband is not mine to relinquish, my dear," he said. "He belongs to Mama. She'd tear us all to pieces if he were to leave now. Tonight is their wedding night. It's all been arranged. You should have left him as you found him. He won't last an hour as a human." As if to emphasize his words, a pounding on the upstairs wall reverberated through the house with terrifying power and insistence. "There, you see?" he said. "Ah, the grandeur of it all. Love knows no seasons."

Christine closed her eyes to the bedlam. This is a madhouse, she thought. Do not go mad. Remember, you have something to do.

Anderson watched her in mock sympathy. "Patience, Christine. You'll get used to her as the years go by. You'll even pace like that yourself someday." He snapped his fingers. Setting his drink down, he stood up and walked to a bookcase in the back of the room. Selecting a tape, he inserted it into a machine on the bottom shelf. Music filled the room, dimming the thudding noise from above. "Die Walküre," he said. "I adore it. My roots are Nordic, you know." He sat down heavily and picked up his drink, spilling half of it.

Good, Christine thought. He's getting drunk. The drunker the better, beast. "Karl," she said. "Then let my son go. Let him walk out of here now and I'll stay with you as long as you like, I swear it." Until I burn you, beast.

Anderson shook his head firmly as if they were bargaining over the price of a curio. "No, no," he said. "No loopholes this time. No imperfections. No, it's impossible. And you needn't look at me like that. You are dealing with a troll in whom the quality of mercy, as they say, is not present."

Christine had to fight to get the next words out. "But you love me. I know you do. That's a human quality, Karl." Keep him talking, she thought. Get him to sit near you.

"A weakness," he said. "A remnant from my father, whom I never saw, thanks to that mantis up there. A confusion. I lust after you, Christine, and think it's love. I don't need your promises to stay with me. You are mine now and will never leave me. In a day you shall be in thrall, eager for my words. In two weeks you shall not care whether your husband and son ever existed. We cannot mate until your entrance into my world is complete. It would produce insanity or death. You could not serve my purposes in either case. But after the moon has filled two times . . . ah, Christine. Even the proud stars shall envy our passions. We shall run the night together. We shall drink at strange fountains, you and I. We shall stand on blue ice mountains and with rime-covered lips shriek the envious stars out of the night sky." He was drinking rapidly now, talking with a careless, expansive moving of his arms. Christine watched him carefully, her lighter clutched in her hand. "I shall teach you joy,

Christine," he said eagerly. "Not your pale, human maunderings, but exultation that bursts the heart. The joy of darkness, the joy of attack. The rumble of the glacier shall be in your throat, and yet, your stalking shall be like a single falling snowflake. All the invisible, potent powers of the earth shall be yours, my Christine. The raw power of a mountain; the splendid force of the tides; the stealth of cats shall enter your loins; you shall run on the wind; all the magnetic power of the earth itself shall course in your veins." He rose to his feet clumsily, upsetting the pitcher on the table between them. He walked unsteadily to the fireplace and returned with a thick metal poker in his hand. He stood in front of her. "The powers of the earth, Christine," he said. He twisted the heavy metal between his hands until it parted like hot wax.

Oh, my God, Christine thought. He's showing off. She hid the lighter under her leg.

Anderson began to lead the music with the twisted metal, his eyes closed. "The Valkyrie, Christine. See them streaming across the sky. We shall run before them, you and I, flaming like comets. Ah-h-h. The gods are dying, Christine. It is written in the Edda. It cannot be changed. Ragnarok is coming!" He threw the metal down and raised his hands toward the ceiling. "It is coming. That final battle between the gods and the giants. And this last battle the giants will win. The serpent of the Midgard, oh my dragon, will swallow the sun. The world will return to chaos and darkness and ice from whence it came." He pointed a wavering finger toward the window. "See how dark the sky gets,

Christine. It is they, my giant companions. Buri, Wachilt, Weland. They fill the night. Geirrod, Hidimbas, Stalo, Thjazi. The sky will be black with their shoulders. We are multitudes, Christine. Multitudes waiting to be free again. Every volcano is a fire giant imprisoned in the earth, belching the hatred of his vitals toward the heavens. Every tidal wave sloughs off the back of a sea giant as he writhes in the ocean's depths to be free. Every earthquake, every crumbling glacier is a fire giant, a frost giant, awakening, stretching, preparing to pull down the firmament and those who rule it. Join us, Christine. Enter the winner's circle. In the eons to come the trolls and giants shall rule the world." One finger went shakily to his lips. "Do you think we are alone, Mama and I?" He shook his head. "There are trolls everywhere, everywhere. A secret, hidden race whose time is not yet come. They're in the trunks of trees you pass in the park. Joggers beware. They live under the snows of every high mountain in the world. Skiers beware. Beware the gluttonous ones who live burrowed in garbage dumps. Doubly beware the thin ones who dwell in the drain pipes of houses. There are trolls, huge and hairy, who live in ice caves, and brown, desiccated trolls who inhabit sand dunes. And then there are trolls such as yours truly, with a long line of human ancestors. Charming people, really. Neighbors like myself. Fixing cars, painting houses, borrowing a pinch of salt. Falling in lust. Each of us with one thing in common. We all hunt in the dark. We shake your house at night as we hurry by. Our disappointed cries are heard on bright city streets, our hunting roars mix with the thunder."

Anderson was standing directly above Christine now. She hardly heard what he was saying. Her mind was intent on a single thought. Sit down beside me, beast, so I can set you on fire.

"Ah," he said, peering drunkenly down at her, "I've frightened you with my meandering. How pale you are. Shall I join you and whisper sweet things in your ear to bring the blush back to your cheeks? Such sweet things, Christine."

Do it, she thought. Christine looked up at him steadily. "I don't see how I can stop you, Karl," she said.

He sat down at her side. Christine looked directly at the shining, swollen features, into the eyes that were like endless circles of pale blue fire. His fetid, drunken breath caused her to blink as his head moved toward her ear. Do it now, she thought. No matter how pathetic, how useless it seems. Try it now. The beast wants to kill your son. She withdrew the lighter from beneath her thigh and held it, behind his back, under the end of his blazer.

Anderson began talking in a low, surprisingly gentle voice. His words entered Christine's consciousness like secret, singing arrows. She tried to press the lighter but she did not. She listened. Her eyes fluttered and closed. As his words continued to flow into her, she felt warm, excited. A glow and terrible ecstasy permeated her being. Primordial melodies echoed in the dark regions of her brain. She smelled perfumed winds. Drifting in rainbowed mists, towering sylvan cliffs swarmed with pterodactyls calling her name. Christine. Christine.

She wrenched her eyes open. Still lying on the floor, his face etched in pain, Nick called her name again. She turned her head toward him and saw him glance at the lighter in her hand and nod his head slightly.

God, Christine thought. What happened? She shouted her son's name to herself over and over again, drowning out Anderson's continued murmuring. She heard the soft click as she pressed the lighter behind Anderson's back.

The lighter did not work. In utter panic, she pressed it again. There was no flame. The lighter did not work.

She heard Anderson's voice stop. As in a dream, she saw him turn his head and look down. She saw him leap up and knock the lighter from her hand as he did so. In a dream that was close to death, she heard a snarl escape his lips of such savage intensity that it shook the walls of the room. She closed her eyes as if in sleep. End the nightmare, beast, she thought. End it quickly.

"Treachery!" Anderson's voice roared. "Fucking, treacherous slut!" He stamped his foot in rage, cracking the floorboards, plunging his leg through to his knee. Christine's eyes opened at the sound. She watched in fascination, unable to bear her fear any longer, as he pulled his foot out slowly. His sudden rage appeared to have left his face but his eyes glowed redly as he absently brushed his pant leg and stared at her. "Now, Mommy," he said flatly, "it's my turn."

He walked over to Joey, pulled him roughly out of Nick's grasp, and returned to the couch.

Something broke within Christine. She flung herself at Anderson, her fingers reaching for his eyes. Without looking at her, he pressed her back onto the couch and held her there. With his other hand he placed Joey on his knee, gazing at him almost fondly. "And now, Joseph," he said, "Mommy is going to watch us play a little game. Let's see, what shall we play?"

Writhing helplessly, Christine's anguished eyes fell on Nick. He was inching himself along the floor toward the discarded lighter that had slid to the fireplace hearth. She watched as he reached it and crawled painfully toward the window behind him. Anderson, his back to Nick, had his hand firmly implanted in Joey's dark hair. Joey pushed at it unsuccessfully, his mouth drawn down in fear. "Lemme go," he cried. "Lemme go!"

Anderson shook his head. His mouth was smiling, but his eyes were twin suns. "Not until we've played our game. What *can* we play? Do you like to play horsey?" His knee began to move rhythmically up and down. "You're not a very good rider, are you, Joseph. I'll have to help you." His grip tightened on the boy's hair. The knee began to move faster, up and down, up and down.

Christine was staring past the terrified figure of her son at Nick. She watched as he reached toward the drapery that hung to the floor beneath the window. She saw him click the lighter once, twice, and then she saw the tiny flame. Dazedly, she watched the ancient material start to burn with a small, stuttering flame.

"I know what we can do," Anderson's voice boomed out. The pupils of his eyes were scarlet. "We shall reenact 'The Legend of Sleepy Hollow.' Now, I'll be the horse. And your mother, she can be foolish Ichabod Crane. Now, we've got to scare her very much. Let me see now," he bit his lower lip, "how are we going to do that?" His eyes lifted slowly to Christine's.

Behind him, Nick raised himself on one elbow. "Bastard," he called hoarsely. "Turn around."

Anderson whirled, letting Joey slide to the floor. The flames had engulfed one side of the draperies already and were licking toward the other side and the ceiling.

Anderson's scream paralyzed Christine, shook her being. It was like nothing ever heard on earth. It did not belong there. It was the sound of some monstrous, cosmic pig being unwillingly led to slaughter. Squeal after ear-shattering squeal rent the air, breaking the windows, attacking the sanity of the people within the room. Anderson's terror did not allow him to run. He stamped both feet repeatedly, once again splintering the floor beneath him. He picked up the table in one hand and threw it at the flames, then a lamp, and then some pieces from the broken floor. As Anderson's panic increased, Nick rose unsteadily to his feet and proceeded, methodically, to set fire to the rest of the drapes in the room. Anderson's head followed him in horror. His screams became louder, more high-pitched. He tore at his clothes, pulled clumps of hair from his head. He lifted his face to the ceiling above him. "Mama!" he shrieked. "Save me! Bestla! Bestla! Save me!"

An answering cry, like a thunderclap, came from above. "Jotunn! Jotunn!"

As the room slowly became an encircling inferno,

peal after peal of stark terror emanated from Anderson's throat. Nick walked past his unseeing eyes, gathered Christine's hand in his good one and helped her up. Joey clung to his belt. Dazed, staring at the apparition in the middle of the room, they ran into the hall and then out the front door.

They raced along the black-topped driveway toward the station wagon, their faces twisted in private visions of terror. When they reached the car, Christine and Nick looked back momentarily at the house. The bottom floor was filled with fire. Flames surged out of the windows, casting an eerie, crimson glow into the fog. Anderson's squeals fractured the warm evening air. The volume was still unbearable.

Nick's eyes were fixed on the upper stories of the house, the lines of his face drawn taut. "Let's get out of here. Now. Chris, you'll have to drive."

Christine stood by the car shaking. "I can't, Nick," she said breathlessly. "I can't." She looked into his stern, steadfast eyes. "All right," she said finally. "I'll try."

Even as he slid into the car Nick's gaze never left the house. As Joey climbed onto his lap, Christine saw his eyes close momentarily in pain, but when they reopened they were fierce and steady. "Let's go," he said. "Let's get the hell out of here."

Christine saw the look on his face. "What is it, Nick? They're going to die, aren't they?"

"Yeah." Nick's voice was not convincing. His eyes were unblinking, expectant. "Let's go, Chris," he said.

Unnerved by Nick's tone, Christine pumped the gas

pedal several times. She turned the key. The car whirred and coughed. It did not start.

"Damn! Damn! Damn!" Christine exclaimed in panic. She struck the steering wheel with her palm. "Damned car!"

Nick placed a quick hand on her arm. "Easy, honey," he said. "Try it again."

Christine tried several more times without success.

"It's flooded," Nick said. "We'll have to wait a few minutes before you try it again." He resumed staring back at the house.

There was a loud popping noise, a wet bursting. The squealing stopped.

"What was that?" Christine asked.

Nick did not turn his head. His eyes were grim. "The bastard's gone." he said. "Fire does not treat trolls well at all." He spoke with satisfaction.

Christine rested her forehead on the steering wheel. "Nick," she said in a tired voice, "is it over? Tell me the nightmare is over."

Nick's eyes remained unwaveringly on the house. One hand absently stroked Joey's head, which was nestled in his shoulder.

When Nick did not reply, Christine lifted her head to look at him. "What is it, Nick?" she said. "What are you looking at?" She followed his gaze toward the house.

The answer was not long in coming. An entire section of the roof burst apart in a huge shower of sparks. Trailing long white hair behind it, a gigantic figure rose through the fire-crimsoned fog like a creature spewed forth from the bowels of hell. It landed on its feet ten yards from the car.

Christine screamed. Nick and Joey sat frozen, their faces transfixed by what they saw. There on the driveway stood Karl Anderson's mother. She was over eight feet in height. Her hulking, muscular body rose to a huge neck and a small head. Her white hair streamed down to her waist. Her face was an amalgam of horror. Mrs. Anderson's perfect nose, brow, and mouth were compressed into the tiny face, whose complexion was blue, speckled with gray. Two huge tusks surged upward from the lower jaw, almost to her eyes, twin maniacal orbs of pure fire. Her entire body was mottled with gray and blue, and was sparsely covered by long wisps of white hair. Three rows of long, black dugs issued from her chest and abdomen. Her taloned hands hung almost to the ground.

She took several steps toward the house until her fear of the curling flames stopped her. "Jotunn!" she called in a voice that was more an animal cry than human. "Jotunn!" The small head twisted back and forth. She pulled at her dugs in anguish and stamped her feet. And then she opened her mouth and roared. The sound of raging thunder filled the night. With each roaring bellow her head swelled and then returned to its previous size. She stalked along the side of the house uprooting shrubs and trees and hurling them toward the flames. She returned to the driveway and wrenching up the cobblestones cemented along its edge, flung them like pebbles. As each stone struck the house, it pierced the walls in a flurry of sparks. Her roaring never ceased. In her impotent rage, she held a stone in either hand and rubbed them together until they glowed red. Then she threw them at the house—red, glowing comets. She stood in the driveway and stamped her feet, sinking deeper and deeper through the blacktop and the earth beneath it.

Nick, struggling to keep the fear out of his voice, touched Christine gently on the shoulder. "Chris, start the car," he whispered hoarsely. "Try the car."

Christine shook her head helplessly, her mouth open, her eyes riveted on the creature in the driveway.

"Do it, Chris," Nick said, shaking her shoulder.

Her expression unchanged, like someone in a trance, Christine turned the key. The starter whined loudly. She tried it again. The car did not start.

The roaring stopped abruptly. The silence that followed brought fresh terror to Christine's face. Her eyes were irresistibly drawn toward the creature in the driveway.

The small head was turning in her direction. Out of the fog, the eyes of fire stared directly into her own, bringing chaos to the furthest reaches of her soul, to the marrow of her bones. The tusked mouth opened. A rushing sound, like far distant waterfalls, reached her ears. It grew in volume, limitless, black astral winds howling in darkness, until it became a thousand voices screaming madness. The troll began methodically freeing her feet from the blacktop. She stretched one hand toward the car.

"Mommy!" It was Joey's voice weak with fright. In reflex to his cry, Christine turned the key again. The car sputtered and almost caught.

The troll's feet came free. She started toward them with silent footsteps, flowing like a powerful, uncoiling snake. The perfect, old woman's mouth still hissed its boundless rage.

Christine turned the key again. The engine coughed agonizingly long and then roared into life. Hardly aware of what she was doing, she put the car into gear and it lurched forward.

Christine drove quickly down the long driveway. The further away they got from the hellish thing standing behind them, the more she began to feel again, and to react again. Fear flooded her body, trembling her hands against the wheel. Hysteria rose up within her like the wild notes of an insane soprano. She slowed down. She had almost gone off the road. She switched the headlights on. They cut through the fog in front of her, yellowing it, making it almost palpable.

"Mommy, no!" Joey's voice was a scream of fright. Christine looked into the rearview mirror. Far back in the driveway, the troll was running after them, her legs working like two smooth pistons. Her small head was thrust forward intently, the tusked jaw clenched shut.

Nick was looking back through the rear window, his face drained of color. He grabbed Christine's arm, hurting her. "Drive it," he said.

"Nick, I can't, I . . ."

"Damnit, Chris, drive it. Put it to the floor or she'll kill us all."

Christine pressed the gas pedal down. The car sped forward through the swirling, thickening mist. When she reached the main road to town, she slowed down, made a screeching turn and then picked up speed again. She glanced at the speedometer. It said forty-five miles an hour. "Nick," she gasped, "we made it. We made it."

Nick sat like a statue, staring at the fog-shrouded road behind them. Several seconds passed. When he spoke, it was in a voice that Christine did not recognize. "Oh, sweet Jesus," he whispered.

Looking in the rearview mirror again, Christine saw the troll in the road behind them. She was advancing on the car with steady strides, the thick neck thrust forward in intense concentration. Christine pushed the gas pedal down further. The speedometer read fifty, then fifty-five. She had difficulty staying on the winding road. The car swerved and bucked. The troll's head lowered with the effort as she gained on them with every stride. In another mile she was directly behind the car. In the mirror, Christine's brief glance caught the white hair streaming behind the troll's head, her neck swelling like a bellows, the jaws snapping in the tiny face of terror. In another moment the troll was alongside the car. With a bestial roar that nearly paralyzed Christine's mind and body, the troll seized the luggage rack with one hand and placed her feet on the rear bumper. She stretched along the top of the car, pounding with gigantic blows of her free hand on its roof. The metal began to buckle from the repeated hammering. She began to roar again in her rage and frustration, great shattering squalls of unspeakable abomination.

Christine swerved the car to the right and left in an

effort to shake her off. The pounding continued. We're dead, she thought. Joey, Nick, and Christine. We're dead. Hatred for the thing above them welled up within her, scattering her fear, clearing her mind. If we go, you go, beast, she thought. I'll turn the car over, hit a tree. I'll kill you. I'll . . .

Her mind stopped racing as a sudden thought struck her. The bridge! The bridge! Get to the bridge! The tracks will sweep her off!

Less than a half mile ahead of them the road passed beneath an unused railroad bridge. There were huge rock foundations on either side. The fogbound road was straight now. Christine increased her speed to sixty miles an hour.

As the dark bridge loomed in front of them, Christine's mouth opened in dismay. Oh, no. God, no, she thought. It's too high. If she's lying on the roof, she'll pass right under it. Just then Christine heard the sound of metal being torn apart. The roof! A painful thrill of terror bolted through her. Joey! She's breaking through. Joey! Christine could feel the sudden rush of damp night air on her neck.

A desperate idea flashed through Christine's mind. She rolled down the window at her side. She screamed into the night. The effort tearing her throat, she screamed again. Within seconds the troll's head hung down by the window. The head and neck were reared back as if ready to strike. Christine veered the car to the left. An instantaneous and ear-shattering cacophony of sound surrounded them: the rending of metal, the breaking of glass, the squealing of tires. Christine struggled to maintain control of the careening car. The splattering thud of flesh against stone was lost amid the strident bedlam that reverberated around the stone-encased tunnel.

The ruined car flapped to a rough stop on the other side of the bridge. It was listing to the left on two flat tires. Christine stared at her hands on the steering wheel. She was surprised at how steady they were. After a brief moment, she looked at Nick and Joey. Nick was staring out the rear window in disbelief as he pressed Joey's face to his chest. The impact had caused the troll to all but disappear. It was as if some malignant, unquenchable rage had burst the body from within. Shards of flesh, splinters of bone lay strewn about the road. The rock walls were covered with dark blood. There was nothing else.

Slowly Nick turned his head and looked into Christine's face. She saw many things there. For the first time since she had known him, there were tears in her husband's eyes.

Christine began to cry quietly. She felt nothing, she felt too much. She could not arrange her face. Gently, she kissed the shattered hand that lay folded helplessly across his chest. Softly, she pressed her face against his shoulder.

It was Nick who spoke first. "Chris," he said, his voice low in wonder, "you did it. Oh, my, you really did it, Chris." He kissed her cheek tenderly. "No more bad dreams. No more. It's over, my darling, Chris. The beasts are dead."

28

The early morning sun had begun to burn the fog away. Dark cedars, with their droplet tiaras, began to emerge along the shoreline. Bronzed patches glimmered in the gray waters of Mill Harbor. The sailboats lay motionless, great dawn-pink seabirds, on the misted surface. Only the tops of the tall reeds stirred, waving gently in the wake of the departing night.

In the unbroken silence of the house, Christine watched the darkness disappear, watched incuriously as the familiar shapes in her bedroom began to form.

She had not slept nor closed her eyes. She was

remembering. She remembered vaguely the hospital where Nick's collarbone had been set. He was going to require special surgery to restructure his hand. Henrietta, battered but indomitable, had been placed in the intensive care unit. She was suffering from shock and a broken shoulder, but the doctors had said she would recover in time.

Vaguely, she remembered the police station, where Lieutenant Broderick and two other detectives had questioned them for over an hour before departing in a squad car for the railroad bridge and the boathouse, unbelieving but polite. She remembered so many things. Events and sequences blurred. And then, bursting in her mind with terrific utter clarity, visions, sounds. Joey bouncing, wide-eyed, on Anderson's knee, the great hand clenched in the dark hair. Henrietta's mascaraed, upside-down eyes. A squeal that seared the brain. A small head tensed backward at the car window. Joey's face as he slept through this night, furrowed like a newborn baby about to cry.

Christine lay there, remembering. Finally, she closed her eyes. She did not sleep.

In the boathouse, still partly hidden by the fog, snakes slithered restlessly among the foundation stones and along the floor, excitedly searching. A passing vixen stopped and turned her head toward the sound, her eyes bright and wild, her mouth open in fox smile.

The mailbox at the end of the Anderson driveway glinted dully in the sun. Beyond it the charred remains of the house stood silently beneath the blackened trees.

The fire engines were gone now, but their clangor seemed to remain in the air, captured in the acrid smell of the wet, burned wood. Beneath the mailbox, a long black snake glided upward along its base. Its tongue, with delicate anticipation, flicked toward the unread letter within.

Jotunn,
Your recent letter disturbs me. It looks like you will have to move again. Indiscretion, Jotunn, indiscretion is your nemesis always.

This professor you describe. This writer of reports, this troublemaker. He must not be allowed to perpetuate his tales. Chastise him, Jotunn. Chastisement is in the air. I live fifty miles away but I can smell it from here. You have perhaps waited too long.

You are too easygoing in these matters, Jotunn. You should have acted immediately. I would have. You know me. I do not have your sunny disposition, your good humor, and easy ways. But my chastisements are always prompt and eternal. You have always labeled me vindictive and terrible-tempered. I am merely efficient. I do not allow reports to reach policemen's desks, as you have.

But that is the past. If I do not hear from you in the next few days, I shall pay you a visit. If you have not punished this man, and anyone else who threatens your well-being, I shall take it upon myself, as I have in the past, to do it for you. You know the fulfillment these activities bring to me. And after all, my brother, what are families for if not to help one another? Blood is thicker than water, said the spider to the spider, if I may be permitted a frivolity here.

How is our precious mother? The very thought of anyone trying to harm you or our beloved Bestla fills me with a rage I find difficult to suppress even as I write. How I miss her. If you have to move, be locally vindictive and then move here. We shall be a family again.

And, Jotunn, the hunting is superb.

Hyrmgar